"It's a good thing we're not interested in each other."

As soon as the words were out of his mouth, Dalton berated himself. *Liar.* He *was* interested. He couldn't deny it.

"That's what I told my mother," Erica replied.

He should be relieved, but regret was all he felt. She didn't like him the way he liked her.

"Look, your mom is right. Our relationship is complicated enough. You're my boss. You were married to my ex-wife's husband. We both have kids. I'm glad we get along, but we both have too much to lose by even thinking beyond our current relationship."

After a deep inhale and a loud exhalation, she nodded. "You're right."

As she snuggled back into the seat, he frowned. She seemed perfectly content with them being friends. And he should be content with it, too. But the extra time together getting ready for the Christmas event could tip his heart in the direction he didn't want it to go. And then what would he do?

He needed to lock down these feelings before he got hurt.

Jill Kemerer writes novels with love, humor and faith. Besides spoiling her mini dachshund and keeping up with her busy kids, Jill reads stacks of books, lives for her morning coffee and gushes over fluffy animals. She resides in Ohio with her husband and two children. Jill loves connecting with readers, so please visit her website, jillkemerer.com, or contact her at PO Box 2802, Whitehouse, OH 43571.

Books by Jill Kemerer

Love Inspired

Wyoming Legacies

The Cowboy's Christmas Compromise

Wyoming Ranchers

The Prodigal's Holiday Hope
A Cowboy to Rely On
Guarding His Secret
The Mistletoe Favor
Depending on the Cowboy
The Cowboy's Little Secret

Wyoming Sweethearts

Her Cowboy Till Christmas
The Cowboy's Secret
The Cowboy's Christmas Blessings
Hers for the Summer

Visit the Author Profile page at LoveInspired.com for more titles.

The Cowboy's Christmas Compromise

Jill Kemerer

LOVE INSPIRED

INSPIRATIONAL ROMANCE

LOVE INSPIRED®
INSPIRATIONAL ROMANCE

Recycling programs
for this product may
not exist in your area.

ISBN-13: 978-1-335-59698-7

The Cowboy's Christmas Compromise

Copyright © 2023 by Ripple Effect Press, LLC

For questions and comments about the quality of this book, please contact us
at CustomerService@Harlequin.com.

Love Inspired
22 Adelaide St. West, 41st Floor
Toronto, Ontario M5H 4E3, Canada
www.LoveInspired.com

Printed in U.S.A.

Peace I leave with you, my peace I give unto you:
not as the world giveth, give I unto you. Let
not your heart be troubled, neither let it be afraid.
—*John* 14:27

To all the single parents trudging through a busy holiday season. You've got this. And to Shana Asaro and Rachel Kent for making this series happen. Thank you!

Chapter One

Yes, she was desperate, but was she *this* desperate?

Erica Black turned down the radio's volume as she pulled into the parking lot of the feedstore. Only three days into November and she'd already heard "Rockin' Around the Christmas Tree" twice on the drive here. At least Rowan wasn't in the back seat crooning "Wock, twee!" this go-round. Her two-year-old son was back at the ranch with Gemma Redmond. That woman was a blessing from the Good Lord Himself. What Erica would do without the housekeeper/babysitter, she couldn't—and wouldn't—contemplate. As it was, she had enough on her mind to occupy the next thirty years.

One problem in particular had risen to the tippy-top of the list, elbowing all the others aside. She needed to hire a ranch manager. Every candidate she'd vetted over the past two weeks had either been unsuitable, unqualified or unwilling to move to Jewel River, Wyoming.

Which left Dalton Cambridge.

She maneuvered the extended-cab truck into an empty spot. The parking lot was almost deserted seeing as it was Friday and nearly closing time. As she climbed down to the pavement, Erica shivered in the wind, then slammed the door. With long, confident strides, she made her way to the entrance. Her phone started chiming rapid-fire, and she took a moment to scan the screen. Two texts were from her ex-husband, Jamie, wanting to pick up Rowan an hour late tomorrow morning. She snorted. Big shock there. He was supposed to pick up Rowan on Fridays and had already pushed it to Saturday this weekend.

Her ex-husband routinely expected special accommodations regarding their visitation schedule. Well, she'd bent over backward for him their entire marriage, and the instant she'd found out he was cheating on her, she'd abruptly ended her policy of letting him have his way.

She wasn't changing tomorrow's pick-up time again.

There was also a text from her mother asking if she had plans tonight. Her mom worried about her and wanted her and Rowan to move back to the family ranch in Sunrise Bend.

Wasn't happening. Especially now that Erica had inherited Winston Ranch from her great-aunt. Nope, she was embracing her future in Jewel River.

The final text was from her sister, Reagan. I just landed in Denver. I start tomorrow. Chocolate and heart emojis followed.

With fingers trembling from the cold, Erica quickly texted back. You're going to be great! I'm so proud of you!

Reagan was finally doing something for herself. She'd taken a temporary position in Denver at a candy store to learn how to make handcrafted chocolates. Erica kept trying to convince her to move to Jewel River. Maybe her sister could open a chocolate shop here. It would be great to be together again.

Erica slipped the phone into her purse, opened the

door and walked inside. Warm air and the scent of grains welcomed her. If Reagan knew what she was up to at the moment, what would she say? Probably something along the lines of "don't worry, it will all work out."

Would it, though?

A lone customer milled about, and she hoped he wouldn't linger. She'd purposely timed this visit to coincide with the store's closing hours.

The opening chords of "Rockin' Around the Christmas Tree" spilled through the speakers, instantly putting her on edge. Being here was difficult enough without her least favorite Christmas song blaring through the sound system.

Maybe she should leave. It would make the long drive here a complete waste of time, but so what? This errand had surely been doomed from the second she'd gotten the idea, anyhow. The more she thought about it, the more ludicrous it sounded.

Hiring her ex-husband's new wife's ex-husband to manage the ranch? *Wait…* Frowning, she mouthed the words *ex-husband's new wife's ex-husband…* Was that even right? Jamie had recently married Haley, who used to be married to Dalton. Erica figured that made them their exes' exes.

This was too convoluted to consider, wasn't it? Exes of their exes?

A tall man with wide shoulders came into view. He didn't notice her as he moved behind the counter to wait on the customer. Her pulse fluttered in the base of her throat. She recognized Dalton from the pictures she'd stalked on Haley's social media before the woman took them down.

With short dark hair and wearing a plaid button-down with jeans, he was undeniably handsome. His hooded eyes—she couldn't make out the color—and sharp jawline gave him a cowboy vibe reminiscent of her two brothers, Jet and Blaine. For some reason, it bolstered her courage.

She was used to dealing with ranchers and cowboys. But dealing with guys like her ex? The spoiled, wealthy man had tied her into knots and made her forget who she was. And she would never let that happen again.

Dalton rang up the sale, and as soon as the customer turned to exit, Erica plastered on a smile and strode forward. Dalton's gaze met hers, and she noted a flash of surprise, then wariness, before he shuttered his emotions. Only the slight flexing of his lightly stubbled jaw hinted at his reaction.

Yeah, well, she wasn't loving this, either.

"Dalton Cambridge?" She thrust out her hand as soon as she reached the counter. "Erica Black."

"I know who you are." He stood there without moving. A steel beam would have been easier to bend. "Whatever you want, I'm not interested."

"But you don't know what I want."

He reached under the counter and popped back up with a binder in his hand. He proceeded to leaf through it as if she wasn't there.

"Could I have five minutes of your time?" she asked.

He flicked a glance her way, then returned his attention to the binder. "No."

"Three?"

He looked up through lowered lids, and hostility practically shot out like a laser beam from him.

"Come on." She kicked her smile up a notch. "Three minutes."

No answer.

"Why not?" she asked. Those two words had gotten her

into a lot of trouble over the years, yet she couldn't stop herself from uttering them.

Dalton slapped the binder shut and looked her straight in the eyes. His were a rich, dark brown, and they glinted with irritation. Refusing to be intimidated, she stood her ground. And he didn't back up a hair.

"I'm not doing this." The words were crisp.

"But you don't know why I'm here."

"I want nothing to do with anything or anyone involving my ex-wife."

"Good, because I don't, either." They were on the same page about that. "It's about my ranch."

His forehead wrinkled, and it looked kind of adorable. Hard to describe a tough case like him as adorable, but it was the truth. His expression reminded her of Rowan when he tried to fit one of his toy tractors into an already full bin.

"If you need advice, ask someone else," he said. "There are lots of ranchers who'll help you."

"I don't need advice."

"Look, whatever you're selling, I'm not buying."

"I'm not selling anything."

"Maybe I'm not making myself clear." He pressed both palms on the counter and leaned forward slightly. "I want nothing to do with you."

Well, he was direct. A point in his favor. Tilting her head, she tried to suppress her temper. *I want nothing to do with you or my ex or your ex or any of y'all. But I'm out of options.* With a measure of restraint she didn't know she possessed, she calmly said, "I'm not here for anything personal. I need help on my ranch."

Hope softened his features, only to be replaced with

skepticism. He glanced at the clock above the register, then sighed. "I have to close up. Give me half an hour."

Victory rushed through her veins. He was open-ish to hearing her out. It was a start. "Should I meet you back here?"

"Yeah." Then he began straightening the counter, effectively dismissing her.

Erica didn't care. A temporary dismissal she could handle. She was used to being brushed off. Jamie had perfected the art of it. But one thing she'd always been was tenacious.

With her head high, she strode back to the entrance and out into the parking lot, then got into her truck to wait. Now that he'd agreed to hear her out, her doubts about him resurfaced. The last thing she needed was someone running the ranch who had a chip on his shoulder and wouldn't listen to her.

Was Dalton wrong for the position? Or was his rudeness simply due to the shock of seeing her? She assumed the latter.

Every rancher in the county had mentioned hiring Dalton Cambridge when she'd asked if they could recommend a new manager. He had experience and the heart for tending cattle.

Besides, she never backed down from a challenge, and she didn't plan on changing that today. Dalton didn't want anything to do with his ex, and she wanted nothing to do with hers, either. This wasn't about their personal lives. It was about the cattle. It was about the ranch.

Dalton needed what she had to offer. He just didn't know it yet.

Whatever she had to offer, he wasn't interested. Erica Black was trouble.

"Sorry the place is messy." Thirty minutes later, Dalton ushered Erica into his apartment. It was too cold to talk outside, and he didn't want everyone around here gossiping at the sight of them sitting together in his truck. So he'd invited her over. And immediately regretted it.

As soon as he'd spotted her in the feedstore, he'd known who she was. How couldn't he when her picture had been splashed in the newspaper after she and Jamie had split up? He'd been drawn to the article even though his hammering heart had known nothing good could come from obsessing about his failed marriage and the participants who'd caused its collapse. He'd been helpless to fight it. After all, he'd been dragged into their drama.

Haley had ruined his life. Her and her then boyfriend, now husband, Jamie Black. They'd taken everything that mattered to him, and neither of them cared how it affected him.

Dalton supposed Erica was a victim in all this, too, but she sure didn't look like she was suffering. There was a glow about her that set his heart pounding in a way that reminded him he wasn't dead yet. *So what?* He'd noticed plenty of pretty women since his divorce had been finalized. Attraction meant nothing unless it was acted on. And he wasn't acting on it. Ever.

Erica was more than pretty, though. She had a vitality impossible to ignore. At around five feet eight inches, she was slender, yet curvy. Her brown eyes were expressive, and two dimples flashed whenever she smiled. Long brown hair flowed down her back, and she was wearing a fitted wool coat over a turtleneck sweater, dark jeans and boots.

"Have a seat." He swiped up an empty soda can and used a napkin to clean off the coffee table, then bustled to the kitchen to toss both in the trash. Then he took the briefest of moments to catch his breath, to gain some equilibrium. Unfortunately, it was nowhere to be found, so he returned to the living room.

"Thanks for agreeing to hear me out." She'd taken a seat on the couch and was pulling off her gloves as she crossed one leg over the other.

Hear her out. Right.

There was a reason—he couldn't imagine a good one—for her being here. All he knew was it had something to do with ranching, and he was intrigued. More than intrigued. He missed ranching with every ounce of his being.

"Let's get this over with." He took a seat on the worn recliner and willed his knee not to bounce.

"I understand you grew up on a ranch." She blinked those big Bambi eyes his way, and he had to force himself to toughen up. He would not get steamrolled by a beautiful face again. His ex-wife had been gorgeous, too, and look at how that had turned out.

"My grandparents owned a cattle ranch near Casper. They raised me." He ran his tongue over his teeth, wishing she'd leave. Having her here was dumb. Why had he agreed to meet with her? He couldn't be involved with her. For any reason.

"Are you familiar with Winston Ranch up in Jewel River?" she asked.

"Of course." It was the largest cattle ranch in this part of Wyoming. Dewey Winston was somewhat of a legend. He'd grown a small cow-calf operation into a sprawling ranch by purchasing neighboring land over the years. He also owned the mineral rights to several properties. His funeral two years ago had practically been a state-wide event.

"I recently inherited it—"

"What?" She—Erica Black—had inherited the Winston Ranch? He couldn't make sense of the words. "How?"

"Dewey and Martha were my great-uncle and great-aunt." Her chin rose as her eyes gleamed with fondness. "After my cheating liar of an ex-husband broke his marriage vows and left me and our baby for your ex-wife, my great-aunt Martha invited me to live with her to keep her company. Dewey had died the previous year, and she was lonely."

Dalton doubted he could hide the disdain in his eyes. Her clipped words about Jamie rubbed salt in his own wound. When Haley left him, his life had fallen apart. Whereas, from the sounds of it, Erica's life had gotten better after her divorce.

She'd had a wealthy aunt to lean on.

She'd inherited a successful cattle ranch.

And what had he gotten?

He'd had to sell the small, heavily mortgaged ranch he'd inherited from his grandparents—the one he'd grown up on.

He'd had to move away from his hometown to avoid the constant humiliating whispers of what Haley had done to him.

He'd had to make peace with the fact that he only saw Grady, his three-year-old son, every other weekend instead of every day.

He'd even had to board his horse, Sugarpie, in stables nearby because he couldn't afford a place with land.

After paying child support each month, Dalton could barely afford this dumpy one-bedroom apartment.

His life stunk.

Erica stared at her clasped hands in her lap. "My siblings and I were all named in the will, and I got the ranch. Sonny Bay's been managing it for decades, but his health took a turn for the worse. I knew he wouldn't be able to run it forever, but I didn't expect to lose him so soon. He's having hip surgery next week and retiring."

Dalton shifted his jaw. He could see where this was going. "Don't tell me you want me to work for you."

"I want you to manage Winston Ranch."

He slumped back in the recliner as all the possibilities swam before him. No more working indoors all day at the feedstore. He'd be outside, checking cattle as he rode Sugarpie. Overseeing a thriving ranch.

What breeds of cattle did they raise? How many head? With a ranch that large, they probably had several ranch hands to share the work.

Ranch manager of Winston Ranch. He shook his head in wonder. It would be an enormous step up from his grandparents' small spread.

"Come out tomorrow, and I'll give you the tour." Her smile revealed more understanding than he'd expected. It had the unfortunate effect of settling into his gut, stirring him to want to respond with more respect than he'd shown her previously.

But this was the ex-wife of the sleazy jerk who'd lured Haley away from him. Jamie Black—the man with everything—had stolen Dalton's wife, and in the process, stolen his ranch, his livelihood, his son.

"It's awkward. I get it." Erica's voice cut through his thoughts. "I wouldn't be here if I wasn't desperate."

He studied her for a moment. Man, this woman had the confidence of five United States Marines. Still…he detected the tiniest glint of fear in her eyes. What did she have to be afraid of?

"Why are you desperate?" he asked.

"No offense, but your name was last on my list." She held up her hands, palms facing out. "Everyone I've talked to recommended you, but truth be told, I interviewed all the other possible candidates first."

He believed her, and for some reason, it made this conversation easier to swallow.

"This isn't some cockamamie way to get back at your ex?" he asked.

"No." Those dimples flashed. "Although, I do try to get back at him any way I can whenever the occasion arises."

He chuckled, then berated himself. *Don't laugh. This isn't funny. Don't even think about considering her offer.*

"Look, I can't afford to get this wrong." Her hand gestured in the air as she spoke. "The cow-calf operation is the biggest part of the ranch, but we also raise crops to supplement their feed and run a small feedlot. I have three full-time cowboys and an agriculture specialist half the year."

"Agriculture specialist?" He raised his eyebrows. "Around here we call them farmers."

"Yeah, well, my term is fancier." Her mouth quirked into a cheeky grin, and both her dimples winked. "Just come out and see the place before you make a decision. That's all I'm asking."

"You're used to getting your way, aren't you?"

"You'd think so." Her smile fell.

Hmm…she didn't strike him as the type to back down. But then, what did he know about women? Haley hadn't struck him as the type to cheat. He'd thought love conquered all. He should have known the meager ranch profits hadn't been enough for her. The rural life hadn't been, either. What a fool he'd been.

It was on the tip of his tongue to decline when Erica said, "I have to warn you, the ranch's policy has always been to work on horseback. I plan on continuing it in memory of my great-uncle. It would mean a lot to Dewey to keep with the old ways."

Horseback. Sugarpie. His pulse sped up. What would it hurt just to look at the ranch?

"What time?" He cringed as soon as the words left his mouth. He shouldn't be doing this. Shouldn't be flirting with disaster. Shouldn't be anywhere near Erica Black and the baggage she brought with her.

"Would nine work for you?"

He nodded. Gulped.

He'd take a tour. That was all. Then he'd drive back here to the real world.

There was no way he could accept the job. His relationship with his ex was strained as it was. He and Haley had used a mediator to hash out how they exchanged Grady because Dalton never wanted to be in the same vicinity as Jamie. Pick-ups and drop-offs were done alone.

If Dalton worked for Erica, he'd be bound to see her ex. He might even run into Haley and him together. Dalton couldn't take that chance. His self-preservation depended on staying as far away from the happy couple as possible. A quick tour of her ranch would have to suffice. Under no circumstances could he agree to take the job.

Erica dropped her purse on the entry table later that night and massaged her neck and shoulders as she entered the kitchen. The long drive home had kicked up all kinds of questions, doubts and concerns. Had she made a colossal mistake by inviting Dalton to tour the ranch tomorrow?

"Mama!" Rowan was sitting in his booster seat at the table with Gemma sitting kitty-corner to him. He raised his hands, both full of chicken nuggets, and grinned. Erica hurried to the table and kissed the top of his head.

"Hello, baby. Were you good for Grammy Gemma?"

His teeth flashed as he nodded.

Gemma's expression was full of affection for the boy. "He's my sweetheart, aren't you, Rowie?"

He nodded and bit into one of the nuggets.

"His nap ran long, so we're just now sitting down for supper." Gemma's pretty blue eyes crinkled at the corners. Her hair was more white than blond and was currently pulled back with a clip. In her early sixties, she was full-figured and had the most comforting and supportive personality Erica had ever encountered.

After her husband died several years ago, Gemma had fallen into a deep depression, closed her home day-care center, stopped paying her bills and had lost her house to the bank. Great-Aunt Martha was the one who'd hired her to help with housekeeping and insisted Gemma live in one of the ranch's cabins. When Erica and Rowan arrived last year, the woman had seemed to blossom whenever he was around. It hadn't taken long for Gemma to slide into the role of Rowan's babysitter.

Erica might not have a traditional career, but she had responsibilities that kept her as busy as any full-time job would. As soon as she got the ranch manager situation handled, she needed to get back to dealing with the pole barn. Her great-aunt had specifically tasked her with using the pole barn to start a business from her heart, one that would help the people of Jewel River.

If only she knew what her heart wanted...

"How did it go?"

"As good as can be expected." She sat in the chair across from Gemma and sighed.

"That doesn't sound good. I'm sorry, hon." The woman radiated sympathy.

"Don't be. Dalton agreed to tour the ranch tomorrow morning, but he's…" Erica fought for the right word. Tough? Closed-off? Bitter? "Prickly."

"Oh, dear."

"Fwy, Mama?" Rowan held out a french fry to her. She thanked him and took it. He pointed to her. "You eat."

She couldn't argue with that. She took a bite. "Mmm. This is good. Thank you for sharing."

"Me share." He took an aggressive bite of his nugget.

"Do you think he'll take the job?" Gemma asked.

"I don't know. Probably not." It would be a long shot. And he might be a bear to work with, anyway. He clearly resented her because of the "ex" factor, and she couldn't blame him for that, but how far would his hostility go?

This ranch was hers. The decisions were hers to make. And she couldn't hire someone she thought would undermine her authority. Jamie had undermined her too often to count.

"He might not be the right fit." Erica pointed to Rowan's plate. "Can I have another?"

He nodded, handing her a french fry as he munched on a nugget.

"You'll know the right thing to do." Gemma's expression was so full of trust in her that Erica almost winced.

Would she know the right thing to do? Or would desperation cause her to make a bad move?

"I might have to manage it myself until someone better comes along." Growing up on Mayer Canyon Ranch, Erica had the experience, but she'd played a minor role.

Her father had taught her and her siblings the ins and outs of raising cattle. While it had never been her passion, she at least knew the basics.

"Oh, Erica, I don't like the idea of you managing the ranch." Gemma brushed crumbs off the table into her cupped hand.

"Why not?" She bristled, ready for a lecture. Her large family had never refrained from saying exactly what was on their minds. They had plenty of opinions on how she lived her life. If they thought she was making a mistake, they told her so. It still tended to ruffle her feathers.

"The pole barn. It's all you've talked about for weeks. I don't want to see you running yourself ragged over cows."

She should have known Gemma would understand. "Thanks. I'll figure out what to do with the pole barn. No matter what."

"I know you will. You have that personality. You're a go-getter." She said it like it was a good thing. So many people in Erica's life had made her feel like her drive was a liability.

"Thanks, Gemma. I appreciate it." She began to relax. "It's getting late. Why don't you take off?"

Gemma pushed back her chair and rose. "What time should I come over tomorrow?"

"Would eight thirty work?"

"Of course." She hugged and kissed Rowan goodbye, then headed toward the foyer.

Erica followed her, thanking her as she gathered her big bag and her coat. "See you tomorrow."

As soon as Gemma had made it off the porch, Erica closed the front door and returned to the table to nibble on another of Rowan's fries.

She was already dreading the morning. Dalton was more handsome in person than she'd expected. The few curt words he'd thrown her way were night and day from Jamie's smooth style. She had the feeling Dalton only spoke the truth, whereas Jamie sugared every sentence with a lie.

An honest man—and a cowboy at that—could be trouble. Not for the ranch. But for her heart.

It was a good thing she was only interested in hiring Dalton. He'd deal with the cattle. She'd be free to figure out what to do with the pole barn. No emotions would be involved.

She could never get romantically involved with a guy so tied to her ex.

But something told her it wouldn't be that easy. Life never was.

Chapter Two

So this was Winston Ranch. Dalton stepped out of the truck and took in his surroundings. Snowflakes fell diagonally with the wind, and the temperature was dropping. Miles of pastures, stands of trees and roaming cattle were visible beyond the corrals and buildings. He almost pinched himself at how peaceful and beautiful this part of Wyoming was.

He couldn't let the atmosphere sway him, though. *Take the tour, give Erica your regrets and go home. In and out. Working for her is out of the question.*

Forcing his feet forward, Dalton noted the barns and stables. Solid and well-kept, from all appearances. The grounds themselves were tidy, and he noted with satisfaction that the large, two-story farmhouse had been built some distance away. Employees would be sheltered from encountering Erica's personal visitors, assuming that guests wouldn't come looking for her in the barns. Any interaction between Dalton and Jamie would be unlikely.

The cold air stinging his face reminded him of all he'd been missing while he worked at the feedstore. He took deliberate strides toward the horse pasture, pausing at the fence. Several horses milled about. Sugarpie would be right at home here.

You can't take this job. Not even for Sugarpie.

Everything about this place tempted him, though. His son's sweet face came to mind. Dalton treasured his time with Grady, loved giving him rides on his shoulders, playing with his toy cars, watching cartoons together on the couch. He wanted to give his son the whole world.

The boy changed things.

Dalton took a deep breath and continued onward, ignoring the snow falling around him. His conflicting thoughts twisted around in his mind.

Child support ate up most of his check, and the owner of the feedstore had mentioned cutting his hours soon. Then there were the texts he got at least twice a month from Haley requesting money for things she claimed Grady needed.

Working here would take the edge off his financial troubles. It might even allow him to save some cash and think about his future for a change. He hadn't realized how tired he was of just getting by until this very moment.

Yeah, but he couldn't afford to forget why he had to turn down the job.

This ranch was like a poisoned apple. Enticing to look at. Deadly to take a bite.

He couldn't handle the thought of spotting Haley and Jamie together. Couldn't bear to have to pretend everything was fine if they arrived here, especially if they had Grady with them. The perfect family. *His* perfect family. Taken from him.

He just couldn't do it.

"Oh, good, you made it."

Dalton startled. He hadn't noticed Erica walking toward him. She was wearing work clothes—jeans, a parka, boots and a stocking cap. Less sophisticated than he'd expected. Her dimples were out in full force as she smiled. Took his breath away, or maybe it was the cold wind.

Even if they didn't have exes he wanted no part of, it would be difficult to work closely with a woman this beautiful. But, then again, maybe he wouldn't be working with her much. Haley had shown zero interest in their ranch. Erica might be the same.

"Come on, let's saddle up." She waved for him to join her as she turned in the direction of the stables.

Or not. She seemed eager to be out here.

"You're going to show me around the ranch?" He jogged to catch up with her, surprised she'd want to take him out on horseback with the snow falling.

"Of course. Who did you think was going to?" She tossed him a sideways glance full of questions, but no ill will.

"I don't know. I didn't realize…" Since she'd recently inherited this spread, he'd assumed she was new to ranching. Then again, everyone he knew grew up riding, so he shouldn't be surprised.

"Don't worry—I was raised on a ranch." Erica's eyes twinkled as the two of them strolled along. "Went out every morning with my dad and siblings to do chores, and I worked cattle with them in the summers." They arrived at the entrance, and she slid open the door for him to go inside. He had the uncomfortable feeling he should have been the one holding the door open for her, but it was too late now. "Our horses are stabled here. You probably saw some of them outside."

"I did." The urge to bring Sugarpie here hit him hard. "I have a horse. I'd need to bring her."

"Oh, good! We have plenty of empty stalls. She'll be right at home here. What's her name?"

"Sugarpie." A lump formed in his throat. The horse probably thought he'd abandoned her…as if he could. Before the divorce, they'd spent every day together. And now? Most nights he drove straight to the stables where she was boarded, but with the seasons changing, it was too dark out to ride her, and he hated leaving her there. They'd been a team, and he missed her. "She's a fourteen-hand, sorrel quarter horse."

"I'd love to see her." Erica continued down the long aisle with stalls on either side. High quality but nothing fancy. "She'll get along fine with Murphy. He's a quarter horse, too. Fifteen-hand. Black. Oh, how I love my Murph." The warmth from being out of the elements and the smell of hay gave the stables a homey feeling he recognized and missed.

They chatted about cows and the employees as they gathered the tack to saddle the horses. One of the cowboys—Erica introduced him as Braylen Jones—led two horses to them. Dalton spent a few minutes getting to know the one he'd be riding. Then he admired Murphy, a well-mannered, powerful beast. Once they'd saddled and mounted the horses, they headed down the lane behind the barns as Erica explained the general layout of the ranch.

"Dewey experimented with the cow breeds, and he finally settled on using crossbred and composite bulls. Black and red. The majority of the calves born are black, and about a fifth are red."

Dalton made mental notes of everything she told him, asking questions when additional information was needed. The more she spoke, the more impressed he became—not only with the ranch, but also with Erica herself. She knew her stuff. Knew more than a lot of cowboys he'd worked with, in fact.

Soon they were riding through a pasture toward a group of cattle. Erica chattered loudly the entire way about the crops they raised and how she wasn't sure if continuing the small feedlot of cattle was worth it.

By the time they neared a group of cows, Dalton's heart was burning within him. He felt like he already knew this place, and he marveled at the knowledge Erica shared.

Winston Ranch was the real deal. And he wanted in on it.

"How long did you say you've owned this?" he asked.

"Two months." She kept a grip on the saddle horn. Her regal posture, the wind whipping the hair that escaped the stocking cap and the way she effortlessly knew the answers to everything he'd asked inspired him...and stirred the attraction he'd already been fighting.

This wasn't a spoiled princess. This was a woman to be reckoned with.

"I don't know much about the individual cows," she said. "But Lars and Sam do, and you'll meet them when we get back. Any questions you might have, they'll be able to answer."

He did a slow perusal of the cattle in his sight. They all seemed healthy and content.

Erica nudged her horse toward a trio off by themselves. One of the cows was noticeably thinner than the others. She dismounted and approached them slowly—they must have trusted her since none of them got spooked.

"Hey there, girl," she said in a low, soothing voice as she held out her hand. The cow sniffed it, and Erica stayed in place to set it at ease. Glancing back at Dalton, she shrugged. "She look thin to you?"

"Yeah." He dismounted and ambled up to her. He let the cow get used to him before inspecting her. "She might have an infection, or she might not be eating enough."

"I'll talk to Lars about it." Erica nodded firmly. "Is there anything else you'd like to see before I show you the cabin you'd be staying in?"

Her words snapped him back to reality. If he took the job, he'd be living here, within walking distance to her house and anyone who might stop by.

Like her ex. And his.

"Would housing be included or do you charge rent?"

She hoisted herself back up in the saddle. "Included, of course. We can go back to the ranch office to discuss your pay, the living arrangements and the hours. I, for one, am ready to get out of the cold."

If she would have said those words yesterday, he would have assumed the worst about her, that she was too delicate for harsh Wyoming winters. But now he could see his assumptions were all wrong.

Erica Black was the real deal. Smart, willing to get her hands dirty, unfazed by the cold, dynamic…and absolutely stunning.

In other words, she was one intimidating woman.

They rode back in silence, and for that, he was glad. He needed to turn down this offer. Needed to get into his truck, drive back to real life and forget this visit ever happened.

As much as he wanted to move here and spend his days riding Sugarpie and working with cattle, he couldn't. He'd lost so much in the divorce, and the only things he had left were limited time with his son—which would never be enough for him—and his beloved horse.

He couldn't trust himself to be mature enough to handle the possibility of seeing Haley here. Or Jamie. Or the two of them together.

And he'd have to be a moron to ignore the Erica factor. She wasn't just his type—she was every man's type. He liked to think he'd overcome his weaknesses, but he hadn't. He was attracted to her. It couldn't be helped.

This ranch was perfection. But the circumstances made it impossible. He had to turn her down. Had to. He was barely holding his life together as it was.

"It's been empty for three or four years." Erica ran her hand along the back of the couch as she led Dalton on a tour of the cabin he'd be living in. It was fully furnished and tucked at the end of the drive that connected the barns and sheds. The trees behind it gave it a private feel. "We keep it clean, and Great-Aunt Martha aired it out often."

After they'd taken care of the horses, she'd shown Dalton around the buildings, and then they'd checked out the steers and the bulls before settling into the office to discuss operations. Two of the full-time cowboys had stopped in to introduce themselves and to brief him on how things were run.

Dalton had asked intelligent questions, and she could tell from the cowboys' reactions and body language that they respected him. It put to rest any lingering questions she'd had about hiring him. When she'd mentioned the salary, his eyes had widened for the briefest of moments, but beyond that, he hadn't said much.

"Three bedrooms, huh." He poked his head into each of the doorways in the small hallway, but he only entered the one leading to the primary bedroom.

"Yes. One bath."

"Not a problem. It's just me, after all." His lopsided grin disappeared as quickly as it arrived. He was a little too handsome when he smiled. In fact, this was the first smile she'd seen from him. It was a good thing he didn't do it very often.

Dalton had left the chip on his shoulder back home, and spending the morning together had made her aware of something she hadn't experienced in years.

Connection. An honest connection.

Yes, she was attracted to this man, but it wasn't because of his gorgeous face or chiseled body. It was the quiet, calm strength of a man comfortable in the saddle and at home among the cattle.

Erica backtracked to the kitchen, hoping Dalton would take his sweet time inspecting the other rooms and give her a chance to gather her thoughts.

Could she really do this? Hire Haley's ex-husband? *Awkward* would be a generous description. The situation felt positively cringey.

"Feel free to look around," she called. "I can wait on the porch if you'd like." Since it was still snowing, she would be better off on the porch. The cold air might clear her head and help her think straight.

"I've seen enough." He joined her.

Was that a good thing or a bad thing?

"Well, what do you think? Do you have any more questions?"

"No."

"Do you want the job?"

He hesitated. "No."

Part of her exhaled in relief, and the other part tensed in regret. She'd allowed herself to picture him here. Had begun to hope he'd take the burden of finding Sonny's re-placement off her shoulders. She studied his posture and didn't find any hostility in it. His expression mirrored her thoughts from a moment ago. If she had to guess, she'd say his decision rested solely on the fact that their exes were married to each other.

But she had to know for sure. "Why not?"

He ran his hand up his cheek and over his ear. There was a vulnerability about him she hadn't seen before.

"It's too bizarre." He met her gaze, and a burst of heat flushed her cheeks at the intensity in his eyes. "The bag-gage. Our exes. Look, I'd be a fool not to recognize the opportunity. This place is organized, well-run and im-pressive."

She stood taller at the compliment. "Thank you."

"But the circumstances… I mean…we can't pretend… What I'm trying to say…" He blew out a frustrated breath. "I don't want to be involved with my ex any more than I already am. I have enough drama."

Erica did, too.

"I understand," she said softly. "I'm disappointed. But I understand. Really."

Dalton shifted from one foot to the other. She gestured to the door, and they made their way onto the porch. As he closed the door behind them, she shoved her hands into her coat pockets, her shoulders instinctively climbing to her ears from the chill. The snow was starting to accumulate.

They made their way back in silence to where his truck was parked.

"If you change your mind, give me a call. I'm looking to hire someone within the week." Then Erica held out her hand. "Thanks, Dalton, for stopping by. For consid-ering the job."

His throat worked as he shook her hand. His firm grip sent a burst of emotion through her chest. He would have been the right fit for this place, but she understood his point. In fact, she felt the same.

The idea of hiring him *was* bizarre.

Dalton tipped his cowboy hat to her, got in his truck and started it up. With a slight wave, he backed out and drove away. Leaving her back at square one.

As she strode down the lane to her house, she reviewed her options. She'd have to call Dave Lassette again. He was the last potential ranch manager remaining on her list. She'd left him several messages, but none had been returned.

The thought pushed her to power walk. Maybe the upcoming meeting of the newly formed Jewel River Legacy Club would provide another lead. After she'd inherited the ranch and read Great-Aunt Martha's letter about starting a business in the pole barn, Erica had been stumped as to what to do with it. She'd talked to her family and closest friends. They'd all had ideas, but none of them seemed to fit.

Erica had then shifted her focus to her aunt's wish for her to pick something that would be good for the community. And she'd started making calls, which had led her to asking more than a dozen people to meet for an informal gathering about Jewel River's needs. Several of the people mentioned getting together regularly. They wanted to work together to make the town vibrant again for future generations. Hence, the Jewel River Legacy Club had been born, and they were holding their first official meeting soon.

Erica stamped her feet up each porch step to dislodge the snow, then wiped off her boots on the mat before going inside. After hanging up her coat, she washed her hands and ambled to the living room, where Gemma was holding Rowan on her lap.

"How did it go?" Gemma asked. Rowan wriggled down and ran as fast as his little legs could carry him to Erica. She bent to hug him, kissed his cheek and straightened once more.

"Good and bad." She lowered herself onto the couch. Rowan came up to her with his arms raised, and she lifted him onto her lap, holding him close. "Dalton would be perfect for the job, but he doesn't want it."

"Why not?"

"The exes situation."

Dawning arrived on her face. "Did you tell him the only time you see Jamie is when he picks up the baby?"

Erica's lips twitched in amusement. Rowan would always be a baby in her mind. "We didn't get into it. I don't think it would matter. It's more the idea of the arrangement, I think."

"I'm not following." Her clear blue eyes couldn't see it.

"Working together, being around each other—it would be a constant reminder that our exes left us for each other. To be honest, I'd pushed that aspect of it out of my mind, and it's probably for the best he turned the job down."

She had a feeling she could fall for a guy like Dalton with two snaps of her fingers.

Gemma's forehead wrinkled as she considered what Erica had said. "What now?"

"I have a few options. I'm hoping someone will give me some names at the meeting on Tuesday." Erica stroked Rowan's hair from his forehead as he rested against her body.

"Is Christy Moulten going to be there?" Gemma asked.

"I'm not sure. Cade's on board. Ty seemed iffy." Christy Moulten was a force to be reckoned with, and her two sons, both ranchers, had been a big help to Erica ever since she'd inherited the ranch. She'd called each of them on more than one occasion. Cade, in particular, had helped by giving her three contacts to call about the manager position.

"If she is, ask her." Gemma nodded. "She knows what's going on better than most."

"I don't want the club meeting to be about me finding an employee, though. We all agreed to brainstorm the specific needs of Jewel River. If I'm going to start a business here, I should probably heed their advice." She glanced at the end table. A tablet of paper and a pen sat nearby. She tended to keep them stashed around the house for whenever she got an idea...which was often.

Gemma heaved herself out of the recliner and pointed toward the kitchen. "Want a cup of coffee? I'm getting one."

"Yes, please." Erica glanced at Rowan, who was snuggled on her lap and half asleep, then she checked her phone. Jamie would be here soon. She'd already packed Rowan's suitcase. It was next to the front door, along with his stuffed bunny. Her sweet boy could rest until his dad arrived.

Her mind swirled with all the unfinished business on her plate as Gemma came back in with a steaming mug and set it on the coaster for her.

"Thank you."

"You're welcome." She then took a seat in the recliner and sipped tentatively. "Oh, my, that hits the spot on a snowy day like this."

"It does, doesn't it?"

Gemma let out a contented sigh. "After this, I'm going

back to my place and spending the afternoon watching Christmas movies. I recorded a bunch. I recorded some for you, too. They have an app listing them all, you know."

The woman lived for made-for-television Christmas movies and couldn't grasp the fact that Erica didn't share her enthusiasm for them, not that she'd watched any in years.

"I'm not ready for Christmas movies yet. It's barely November. And I have way too much to do."

"You weren't meant to work all the time." Her gentle voice softened Erica's worries. "It's okay to take a break."

"I like being busy." She took another sip of her coffee. "I don't know how you get the perfect amount of cream in here, but you do every time."

Gemma smiled. "You always say that."

"It's true. I don't know what I'd do without you."

"I don't know what I'd do without you and the baby, either. Ever since you two arrived, I've been feeling back to myself again. I hadn't realized how much I lost after Bob died."

"I'm sorry, Gemma. I know how much you miss him. I think God knew how much the three of us needed each other."

"That He did, Erica." She took another sip.

"Now if He'd fill me in on what to do with the pole barn…"

"Maybe you should reconsider opening another candle shop. You have the experience."

If it had been anyone else mentioning it, Erica would bristle, but Gemma's relaxed manner put her at ease. Instead of defending herself or getting snippy, Erica allowed herself to be honest.

"Mayer Canyon Candles was Mom and Reagan's thing.

I was merely the business side. I don't know how to make candles—and I don't want to learn. A second facility wouldn't make sense." Her sister and mother had started the company several years ago on the family ranch in Sunrise Bend, Wyoming. While Erica had enjoyed her role in the business, candles weren't her passion and never had been. "The main reason I considered it before was because I thought it might entice Reagan to move here. But she's trying something new with the chocolates. All I can say is my Christmas present had better be a giant box full of truffles."

Gemma chuckled. "Whatever you do, I'll be here to take care of our Rowie."

"I appreciate it. But I don't want you being on call all the time. We'll go back to a set schedule like before as soon as I hire someone to manage the ranch."

"Okay, but I'm always here if you need me."

Two sharp knocks on the door startled her. She stroked Rowan's arm and said, "Time to wake up, sweetheart. Daddy's here."

His eyes blinked open one at a time, and he straightened, still groggy. "Daddy?"

"Yep."

He slid off her lap and ran down the hall to the front door with Erica trailing behind him. "We need to get your coat and boots on, buddy."

She opened the door, and there stood the man she once loved. The one she'd sacrificed her own needs for. The one who'd taken everything she'd given, and it still hadn't been enough.

Peering around his tall frame, she noted the running truck. With Haley in the passenger seat. Erica couldn't see the back seat, but they probably had Grady with them, too. A jolt of anger hit her like lightning.

"We discussed this." She crossed her arms over her chest. Jamie's lack of respect for their arrangement never failed to infuriate her.

"You're being ridiculous."

"Am I?" She kept her tone light, not wanting to upset Rowan, but it annoyed her to no end that Jamie refused to uphold his end of their custody arrangement by bringing Haley with him. "A forty-five-minute car ride alone with him wouldn't kill you."

"Stop being such a shrew. It's not about Haley, and you know it."

A shrew? She had names for him on the tip of her tongue, too, but she swallowed them and turned to help Rowan get his boots on. He was sitting on the floor next to the hall closet and doing his best to tug his cowboy boots onto his little feet.

"I think you need your snow boots today, okay?" She reached into the closet and grabbed the pair. "But you can bring your cowboy boots with you if you'd like."

"Okay, Mama." He beamed at her, and her heart melted at his darling face. She helped him into the boots and coat, then picked up his suitcase, while he clutched Bunny under his arm.

"Hey there, are you ready for some fun?" Jamie crouched and held his arms out to Rowan, who launched himself into them for a hug. Then Jamie met her eyes before straightening. "Isn't it time to retire the rabbit?"

"He's two, Jamie." She glared at him. Why he had such an irrational hatred of Rowan's favorite stuffed animal, she'd never know.

"It's—"

"My bunny." Rowan clutched it to his chest, his eyes welling up with tears.

"That's right. And you take care of Bunny extra good this weekend, okay?" Erica bent to give him a hug. "I'll see you tomorrow night."

"'Bye, Mama." His arms wrapped around her neck and he kissed her before going outside with his father. The two of them walked down the steps to the truck. Erica cast Haley another glance before shutting the door and leaning against it. Every muscle in her body felt tight.

The stunning blonde was everything Erica wasn't.

Poised. Demure. A classic beauty.

No wonder Jamie preferred Haley to her.

It didn't give him the right to flaunt his new wife in front of her, though. The custody arrangement had gotten heated after he'd broken his end of the bargain multiple times, and they'd gone to court to hammer out new rules. They'd agreed to exchange Rowan alone to avoid tempers flaring. She had the legal documents to prove it.

After sliding her phone out of her pocket, she let her fingers hover over the screen as she debated contacting her lawyer.

Once again, her selfish ex was doing whatever he wanted without suffering any consequences.

Sometimes she hated him.

God, I don't mean it. Well, I kind of do. I can't pretend I like him. Honestly, I can't stand him. I don't know how I could have missed all the warning signs when we were dating. And I know You tried to get me to see, but I was too stubborn. Too in love, or so I thought.

She slunk back to the living room. Her mom had warned her about Jamie several times, but had she listened? No. Instead, she'd gotten mad at her mother and stormed off.

And it still irritated her that her mom had been right, while she'd been dead wrong.

"You look upset." Gemma watched her with concern.

"He brought *her* again. I don't care that she wasn't on the doorstep. She's not supposed to be part of the exchange at all."

"Oh, no," she said. "Are you going to call your lawyer?"

She tried to calm herself. "I'll email him on Monday."

In the future, she'd be less trusting and more careful with her heart. She'd given it to a man who didn't deserve it, and she couldn't afford to make a mistake like that again.

Her thoughts went to Dalton. As much as she needed him running the ranch, he'd been right to decline her offer. Him working here would only remind her what she was trying to forget.

Her husband had left her for the perfect woman.

And no matter how hard she tried, she couldn't forgive him for it.

Dalton wished he could forgive Haley. For cheating on him. For leaving him. For ripping him from the only home and work he'd ever known.

For rejecting him.

If he could find a way to forgive her, he'd be able to accept the job Erica had offered. There wouldn't be any reason not to.

Dalton stroked Sugarpie's neck that afternoon as he rode the trails at the stables where she was boarded. The ride had been a necessary balm for his troubled heart. The more he tried to forget Winston Ranch, the more the possibilities grew in his mind.

The cabin was a short walk to the stables. He'd be riding Sugarpie every day, the way he'd done before the divorce. And he wouldn't be dealing with customers or hauling feed bags for eight hours straight. Best of all, he'd be outside, in charge of cattle, doing the very thing he'd been raised to do.

Why had he turned down the job again?

As if to answer his question, his phone chimed. Was it Erica trying to change his mind? He signaled for Sugarpie to halt, then took off his gloves and pulled the phone out of his pocket. He winced when he saw Haley's text.

He read the message and his entire torso stiffened. The woman wouldn't be happy until she bled him dry.

Grady's preschool needs a deposit to hold his spot next fall.

He ground his molars together. Well, maybe her rich new husband could handle the deposit. Wasn't the fact that she took half of Dalton's paycheck enough?

Taking a deep breath, he stared unseeing at the view of snow-covered prairie before him. Then, with his exhalation spiraling in the air, he texted her back. How much?

I need $150.

He gulped, mentally calculating how much he had in his checking account. He couldn't touch his savings—the small amount in there was for emergency use only. Lawyer fees had eaten up most of his portion of the divorce settlement. Costly repairs on his truck had sopped up the remainder.

Dalton patted Sugarpie's neck as he tried to figure

out what to do. He'd just have to take on an extra shift. Except he couldn't. His boss had already warned the staff they'd be getting fewer hours. His chest tightened as anxiety spread.

This was his son. He'd do anything for Grady. If it meant eating canned beans and ramen noodles for a few weeks, he'd gladly make the sacrifice.

Before he could talk himself out of it, he texted Haley back. I'll give you a check when I pick up Grady.

She responded almost instantly. Or Jamie and I can drop him off.

Fury gripped him. He'd been over this with her. He didn't want to see her new husband. At all. Ever.

His thumbs went into overdrive to respond. No. I'll pick him up.

Her reply appeared on the screen. It doesn't have to be this way.

Yes, it did. It had to be this way because she'd cheated on him and then married the guy.

Haley didn't care that it had destroyed him. It must have escaped her notice that while she'd moved on, he was stuck in a run-down apartment, working at a dead-end job and couldn't even be with his son or his horse every day because of her actions.

It *did* have to be this way.

He shoved the phone inside his pocket, aware that his cheeks were freezing and his fingers were growing numb.

And then something clicked inside him. Something profound.

For the first time since Erica had shown up at the store, he actually believed he *could* take the job on her ranch.

The pay was twice what he currently made. Without rent, he'd be able to save a large portion of his earnings.

Sugarpie would be a mere hop, skip and a jump away. He'd be doing what he loved.

Dalton stared at the horizon.

Why couldn't he take the job?

Why couldn't he have a chance at a life he could actually be proud of?

Why couldn't he be the winner for a change?

Clicking his tongue, he urged Sugarpie forward. It was all well and good to think about winning, but reality tended to prove otherwise.

He was getting mighty tired of losing.

Visions of Winston Ranch in all its glory came to mind.

He'd sleep on it. Tomorrow was Sunday. He'd say an extra prayer at church for guidance.

And maybe, just maybe, he'd pay Erica another visit.

Chapter Three

"Come on. Talk to me." Erica held a clipboard as she slowly turned in a circle inside the massive pole barn the following afternoon. If only the space would tell her exactly what its purpose was. It would make life a whole lot easier for her.

Last night she'd caved and joined Gemma to watch one of those romantic Christmas movies. She'd been pleasantly surprised it had kept her attention the entire way through. In fact, she'd gotten a wee bit teary-eyed and had shouted for the guy to "kiss her, already" near the end.

She usually couldn't focus long enough to watch an entire movie. Sometimes, she couldn't sit still long enough for a sitcom. Embarrassing, but true. Regardless, she'd paid attention to the sermon in church today—for the most part, anyway—then had eaten brunch alone at Dixie B's in downtown Jewel River. Weekends without Rowan tended to make her feel lonely.

Instead of wasting time moping, she'd hiked over here, hoping for inspiration. She should have some clue what to do with the barn by now, shouldn't she?

Come on, Erica. You have a degree in finance. You can come up with something.

She'd taken care of the business end of Mayer Canyon Candles, then after getting married, she'd managed one of Jamie's dealerships selling UTVs, boats and four-wheelers. It wasn't as if she had no experience.

But those jobs had landed in her lap. They'd been given to her since she was family.

She strolled across the concrete floor on her way to the kitchen. The petty part of her toyed with turning this barn into a used UTV dealership to directly compete with Jamie's. There was plenty of space for a showroom, and all she'd have to do was add offices and pour the cement for a parking lot out front. She'd be good to go. Zoning shouldn't be a problem since Great-Aunt Martha had pulled permits for it to be a commercial business. However, there were limits to what it could be used for.

It would make Jamie mad, her competing directly with his sales. Would serve him right.

But her heart really wasn't in it. And a business here in little Jewel River would be too far away to compete with the one where he lived, anyhow. Besides, she'd never loved managing his dealership, especially since he'd been constantly on the road supervising the other three.

Erica entered the kitchen and turned on the lights. It, too, was large. A counter with a long pass-through window allowed food to be served. The back wall was lined with empty cupboards. Two massive refrigerators, two stoves and two sinks had been installed. It was ideal for catering. But…she wasn't much of a cook and didn't see that changing in the near future. Or ever.

She meandered back out to the main area. *Think practical, Erica.*

An indoor storage facility would be a no-brainer. It would require quite a bit of construction, but she could see the possibilities. There were two small outdoor storage units in Jewel River, and they were typically at full capacity. She could design hers to be temperature-controlled.

As for Great-Aunt Martha's letter…would it help the community? Yes. But would running a storage facility make her heart sing? No.

Which brought her right back to…nothing. She had nothing.

"Hello? Anyone in here?" Dalton entered the pole barn. He was wearing an unzipped black winter jacket, a cowboy hat, jeans and cowboy boots. As he approached, she noted his clean-shaven jaw and the color in his cheeks. There was a zip in his step that had been missing yesterday.

She didn't want to admit how much the sight of him improved her mood. Smiling, she strolled his way. "What brings you here?"

"I have some questions for you." He stopped a few feet from her.

"Oh, yeah?" She dropped the clipboard down by her side, tilting her head to study him. He could have called or texted. Dare she get her hopes up? "Ask away."

He looked around the space, rotating his neck to take it all in. "What's this? It looks new."

"It is. A little over a year old. And I'm trying to figure out what to do with it. That's why I'm out here."

"Why was it built?" A furrow above the bridge of his nose appeared.

"My great-aunt had the urge to build it after Dewey died."

"The urge to build it." His frown grew more pronounced. "Why?"

"I don't know. She said the reason would come to her. She just knew it needed to be built."

His eyebrows arched. "I cannot relate to that."

"Neither can I." She chuckled. "I'm more of a plan-first, plan-again and plan-once-more-for-good-measure type of gal."

"You don't fly by the seat of your pants?" His eyes creased at the corners, and it made him look younger, less harsh, more approachable.

Dalton was easy to read. Jamie had been less transparent. *Stop comparing. In fact, put Jamie out of your mind altogether.*

"Nope," she said. "That's the opposite of me."

He nodded as silence fell. Erica resisted the urge to move the clipboard to her other hand. She always got fidgety when she wasn't sure what to say.

"Do you want to take this conversation to my house? I can brew a pot of coffee. Gemma—Gemma Redmond is my housekeeper and babysitter—left a loaf of banana bread yesterday. She's an amazing baker." Erica tried to keep her expression neutral. She hoped to hear that he'd changed his mind and was accepting the job.

But…the feminine side of her wasn't sure she should be hoping for that at all. Not when it was a strapping, handsome cowboy she definitely was attracted to.

She'd been alone too long. And ideas had gotten in her head from the movie last night. That was all there was to it.

"I'd like that."

They strode to the entrance together, then out the door and down the path to the house. And the whole way, she couldn't think of a single thing to say. So unlike her. The tension wound up her nerves, and she could only pray she wouldn't blurt out something idiotic like, "Well, cowboy, now that I've got you here, I'm gonna keep you."

He held the front door of the house open for her, and she mentally chastised herself to stop being immature. Obviously, Dalton was considering the job or he wouldn't be here. All she had to do was answer a few questions and have a cup of coffee with the guy. It couldn't be that difficult.

After they'd shed their coats and boots, Erica went to the kitchen and filled the coffee maker with water. "You can park it on a stool or we can talk in the living room. Whichever you'd prefer."

"Here's fine." He rounded the long island and sat on a stool while she scooped grounds into the filter. "Nice place."

"It is, isn't it?" She tossed him a glance over her shoulder. "My great-aunt remodeled it five or six years ago. I love what she did with the place. The only thing I've changed is the living room furniture. Her taste was floral and traditional. Mine is all about comfort."

With the coffee started, she turned to face him, bracing her hands on the counter behind her. The white cabinets and solid-surface countertops brightened the room, and the upper cabinets had glass panels with lights. Erica made a mental note to decorate with holly sprigs this year for Christmas. The dark green foliage and bright red berries would pop against the white and make it festive.

"How often do you see your ex?" Dalton's words sliced through the air, making all her happy thoughts of Christmas decorating run and hide like a prairie dog darting into its hole.

"Um, what?"

"I'm sorry." He lowered his chin. "I just, well…it's kind of important."

Once the initial shock wore off, she realized she didn't mind sharing the details.

"As little as humanly possible. The only time I see Jamie is when we're dropping off or picking up Rowan."

"Same with me and Haley." The mournful expression in his brown eyes tugged at her heart. "Does she come around much?"

It was a sore subject. Very sore.

"Legally, she's not supposed to come around at all. But yesterday, Haley was in the passenger seat of Jamie's truck. I'm not going to lie—it made my blood boil. We went to court about this and specifically agreed to do pick-ups and drop-offs alone. But do the rules apply to my ex-husband? Ooh, no. Never." The words fired out hot and fast, and she sighed. Why had she blurted all that out?

"That's what I was afraid of." He tapped his finger-tips on the counter.

The coffee maker rumbled as it reached the final stage of brewing. Erica opened an upper cabinet and was surprised her fingers were trembling. Shouldn't she be past getting upset over Jamie and his selfishness by now?

She took out two mugs. One said, Happiness is Found on the Ranch and the other said, If You Met My Family, You Would Understand. She filled both mugs and slid the ranch one his way. Then she took the cream out of the fridge and poured a generous amount into her mug before setting the carton in front of him. "Do you take sugar?"

"No, thanks." He read the mug as if it held the answers to the universe.

Hers spoke the truth. She inwardly chuckled at the

thought of her large family. She was a Mayer through and through. Much like her brother Jet, she was stubborn, outspoken and ready to face a challenge head-on.

The man sitting across from her presented a special kind of challenge.

She wanted Dalton to work for her. But she didn't want to get close to him. And her heart was sending out warning flares that this attractive man had the kind of temperament she could easily start depending on for more than his ranching skills.

What was more important? Her sense of equilibrium? Or the success of the ranch?

The ranch.

Always.

"Why'd you really come today, Dalton?"

Happiness is Found on the Ranch. Isn't that why he'd driven out here?

Dalton kept hold of the mug's handle as he tried to figure out how to answer her question. He'd never been a man of words, something Haley had found annoying. He'd never been refined, either. Haley had grown up with money. He'd grown up poor. She'd been teacups and place settings, and he'd been chipped mugs and paper plates. No wonder she'd left him.

But sitting here in this warm, bright kitchen, staring at no-nonsense Erica—who seemed to embrace the unconventional—hope rose so sharply in his throat that it almost choked him.

This. The mug spelled out exactly why he'd come.

Happiness really was found on the ranch.

"I couldn't stop thinking about this place." He could

feel his cheeks starting to burn, so he took a drink of coffee. Anything to not have to meet her eyes.

"That makes me happy." Her smile made her face glow. "I can't stop thinking about it, either. It's great, isn't it?"

This beautiful, energetic woman would be his boss. He might be broken, broke and alone, but he was still a living, breathing guy. Could he really work for her? *With* her? Day after day? Without making his life even more of a mess than it already was?

"It is great." He swallowed, unsure of what he wanted to say. "If it was only the ranch, I would have taken the job yesterday."

"I know." She held the mug between her hands, and he was surprised at the understanding in her expression.

"It's Haley. And Jamie." Their names were bitter on his tongue. "I don't want to run into them."

"I don't, either."

"Working here would increase my chances of seeing them."

Erica angled her head to one side, then the other. She pursed her lips, then conceded, "It would."

"I don't know if I can do it."

"I'd be lying if I said they won't show up here together." She set down her mug and traced the rim. "I mean, we've been to court over this, and Jamie still does things his way."

"That's what I was afraid of." The thought of Haley and Jamie driving up, getting out of their vehicle and wrapping their arms around each other, looking every inch the happy couple, made him sick. He couldn't bear to think of them barging in on his life. Haley and her new husband looked down on him enough already. His work and where he lived would be inseparable if he took this job.

"Are you over her?" The quiet question caught him off guard. Was he over her?

"We were high school sweethearts. I can't remember a time when I wasn't in love with her." It was the truth. He didn't know if he was over her. He didn't even know if it was possible for him to get over her.

"I'm sorry." She sounded sincere. Looked sincere, too.

"So if I agree to take this position, it's with the understanding that I never, ever want to see your ex-husband."

"That makes two of us."

"And under no circumstances do I ever want the four of us to interact."

"It's my worst nightmare." Erica picked up her mug again but didn't take a drink. "I will do anything in my power to avoid it."

He studied her until he felt reasonably sure she meant every word.

"If it helps, Haley always stays in Jamie's SUV. It's not like she's holding his hand all the way up to my porch or anything." She shrugged. "But I can't guarantee she won't at some point. Nothing they do shocks me much anymore."

He'd been afraid of that.

This time Erica did take a drink of her coffee. Then she looked at him. "The only way I can reasonably assure you they won't show up together is if you talk to Haley. Maybe she'll listen to you."

His back stiffened. Talk to Haley? He didn't do that. They texted about Grady. Mumbled hello and goodbye when they dropped off or picked up the boy. And that was it.

"I'm emailing my lawyer tomorrow. I don't know if that helps." Erica nodded thoughtfully, more to herself than to him. "Jamie called all the shots when we were married. Now that we're divorced, I don't jump through his hoops anymore."

Had he jumped through hoops for Haley? He didn't think so. But she'd been good at letting her disappointment show through, and he'd wanted to please her, so he'd done whatever he could to keep her happy.

Maybe he'd jumped through hoops, too, and hadn't realized it.

Maybe he still did.

"I want to work here." He thrust his chin in the air, ready to take a chance on a fuller life again.

"Am I sensing a *but*?" A lopsided grin revealed one of her dimples.

"But I don't want to be around them. I don't want to see them or talk to them. Ever."

Erica appeared deep in thought for a few moments. Then she raised her index finger. "Would it help if you knew our custody schedule? That way you would know exactly when he'd be here. And I can text you when Jamie arrives so you can stay away until he leaves."

"Yes, that would help." His relief was immediate, but short-lived. What she said made sense. If he knew when Jamie was arriving, he could be elsewhere. There would be no reason for him to see them. But his other problem stood a few feet away. How was he going to work with this incredible woman?

"How involved are you with the day-to-day ranch operations?" he asked.

"Not much." She shrugged. "I hope that doesn't put you off. Sonny and I meet every weekday afternoon for twenty minutes or so to go over his checklist. I plan on continuing that with the new manager. But I won't be riding out every day or helping move cattle. We have ranch hands for that. Lars and Braylen rotate on weekends, so you'll have weekends off."

His heartbeat started pounding. Not involved much? Music to his ears.

He could handle talking to her for a few minutes each afternoon. If she wasn't out riding with him every day, he'd be fine. They'd have limited interaction. He could nip his attraction in the bud. Focus on the cattle.

"Well, you talked me into it." He forced a smile, even as his nerves bounced around. Was he making the right decision?

"You're taking the job?" She sounded shocked...and happy.

"Yes." No going back now.

She clapped her hands, and both dimples flashed. "Great! Welcome to Winston Ranch."

The hair on Dalton's arms prickled, but all the benefits of living here flooded him with anticipation. The first thing he would do was load up Sugarpie and get her settled.

The cabin he'd be living in was a big step up from his apartment. He'd be able to take Grady around the ranch, show the boy what being a cowboy was all about.

This job would work out. It would.

He'd just have to be careful. After what he'd gone through with Haley, *careful* was his middle name.

Chapter Four

Tuesday evening, Erica took a deep breath and fought the urge to rub her temples. Besides Erica, fifteen people were seated around long tables pushed together to form a U in the community center. It had taken her ten minutes to get everyone to stop chatting. Now that she had everyone's attention, she was ready to call the first official Jewel River Legacy Club meeting to order.

Clem Buckley, a retired rancher and veteran in his seventies, slapped the table. "We're not doing nothing until we pledge allegiance and open with the Lord's Prayer."

Fine with her. Everyone agreed and got to their feet. Then they faced the flag and joined Clem in the pledge. He led them in prayer, and after a chorus of *amens*, everyone sat down. Erica glanced at Clem and smiled a thank-you. He gave her the stink eye.

What had she ever done to him? She refrained from giving him a dirty look.

"I want to go on record that Jewel River doesn't need outsiders deciding what's best for it." Clem glowered at her full-throttle. His thin, wiry frame, rigid posture, steel-gray eyes and no-nonsense voice made her feel like she was a four-year-old getting scolded.

A few of the older ladies—all active in the community—clucked their approval, which made Erica sit up straight. They all saw as an outsider, did they? At least she was trying to improve the town. It was more than she could say for them.

Christy Moulten—a firebrand in her early sixties—stood and tipped up her chin, giving the entire room a haughty once-over. "Jewel River needs every willing body to get it back to its former glory. And that includes Erica Black."

While Erica appreciated Christy's support, it was clear the group was instantly taking sides. And from the looks of it, they weren't taking hers. It was a good thing she wasn't here to win a popularity contest.

"Thank you all for coming." *Stick to the plan, Erica.* "I know you all care deeply about this community. I do, too. With that being said, let's get started by discussing what Jewel River needs."

The room erupted in loud voices with several people yelling out different things. She winced as she tried to make sense of what was being said. Everyone speaking over each other would never work. She needed to impose some kind of order.

What would Mom do?

Her mother was an expert at maintaining order *and* keeping the peace. Erica was generally less successful at both.

Standing, she took a deep breath, then she put two fingers in her mouth and whistled loudly, the way her dad had shown her.

The room grew quiet.

"Everyone's opinion matters, and everyone will have their say. But we'll be here all night if we're talking over each other. Let's go one at a time. Marc, will you start us off? Then we'll continue around the table clockwise until everyone has a chance to speak. Mind you, we're *not* debating anything at the moment. We're simply writing down ideas."

Marc Young, a local rancher and city council member, thanked her and stood. "As you know, I spend a lot of time downtown at Mom's bakery. It's obvious we need more stores in the empty buildings. Shops and restaurants would help with foot traffic."

"Who's going to shop there?" Clem frowned with skepticism. "We've got a discount store already."

"Excuse me," Erica said, "we're not debating anything tonight, remember?"

"Well, when are we going to debate?" Clem crossed his arms over his chest. "Ideas sound good and all, but if they aren't practical, how will they work?"

"Think of tonight as a brainstorming session." She was this close to losing her temper with the ornery old coot.

His face twisted in a sour expression, but he kept his mouth shut as they continued. Erica took notes on her phone, trying to type as quickly as people spoke.

When Christy's turn came, the stylish woman raised her hands, palms out and fingers wide, and paused dramatically. Her hazel eyes sparkled and chunky bracelets slid down the arms of her red sweater. "The park is in terrible shape. We need a gazebo. Flowers. And a general beautification of the downtown. And don't get me started on the community center." She gave the space a probing look that was full of disappointment. "It smells. Jenna and Braden's wedding reception was almost ruined when the roof leaked last month. Patches and buckets on the kitchen floor are not a solution to the problem. Plus, it's outdated. I doubt this place is up to code, and it's too small for our events even if it is."

"What events?" Clem asked sarcastically. The guy next to him snickered.

"The Christmas bake sale, for one. And we could bring back the spring bazaar—we haven't had one going on ten years now."

"No one wants crocheted doilies." Clem shook his head as if he'd heard enough.

"Who are you to decide that?" Christy popped her hands on her hips.

"Please, no more interrupting." Erica was getting a headache from Clem's negative attitude. Then she smiled at Christy. "Thank you for your input."

Christy gave her cheerful nod, flashed a dirty look Clem's way, then sat down.

Erica turned her attention to Cade Moulten, who was sitting next to his mother. "Cade?"

"Hold up, there, missy." Clem smacked his palms on the table. "Would it be too much to ask you to get off your phone? Your textin' and shoppin' can wait an hour. The future of this town is important to *some* of us."

That did it. This guy had been disrespectful to her all night. She was ready to lay into him.

"That's enough, Clem," Marc said evenly.

Christy leaned over to yell at Clem. "We're all tired of you interrupting."

"I'm speaking common sense. Young people and their idiot boxes," he mumbled. Then he narrowed his eyes at Christy. "And you. If you're not speeding, you're on that phone. If you paid more attention, maybe you wouldn't

have your driver's license revoked every other week."
The instant the words left his mouth, a collective gasp
sped through the air. The entire town knew that Christy
was a terrible driver and had gotten her driver's license
suspended multiple times.

Her face grew red, and she opened her mouth to respond, but Erica beat her to it.

"I'm typing notes in my phone," Erica said. "Not shopping or texting or ignoring you, okay? You owe Christy
an apology."

"Psh." He had the grace to look away. His features
seemed to scrunch together, but he mumbled, "Sorry,"
and that was that.

Thankfully, Cade took it as his cue to speak. Erica exhaled in relief. Cade was respected around here. A natural
leader, involved in the community and handsome as all
get-out. It was a wonder the hunky cowboy in his early
thirties was still single. His brother was gorgeous, too.
Not that she'd noticed or anything.

"We need a veterinarian." Cade's voice commanded
attention. "Bill's retiring soon, and it's going to leave the
entire county in a bind. Every rancher is used to calling
him to come out and help with our large animals. Not
to mention, he had office hours two days a week for everyone's pets. The entire town will suffer if we don't get
a vet here soon."

Erica winced. She'd forgotten Bill Banks was retiring. Winston Ranch had relied on him for years. Cade
was right. They needed a new vet. Pronto.

The meeting progressed. When the final attendee's
turn came up, she realized she didn't know who he was.
The man looked to be in his sixties. He was on the short
side, and his receding white hair was buzzed short. He

had piercing blue eyes and had on a flannel shirt and jeans held up with a belt.

"I don't have anything to add. Just want to say I appreciate us coming together to do some good for this town. I grew up here. Kids and families should have the same kind of life I did when I was young. We all looked out for each other." He sat down again, and silence reigned for several seconds.

Erica made a mental note to catch up with him after the meeting and introduce herself. Who was he?

"Well—" Clem spread his hands wide "—now what?"

Every word this man uttered rubbed her the wrong way. *Come on, don't let him get to you. Channel Mom. She's got to be in you somewhere.*

"Okay, Clem, what do you propose?" Erica asked.

He opened his mouth, then must have thought better of it and shut it.

"I have a suggestion." Marc held up his hand.

"Please share your thoughts," she said.

"It seems all the concerns brought up tonight fall in one of four categories. Some are related to local businesses, others are service-oriented and still others relate to quality of life. Then there are the ones that don't fall into any neat category. Why don't we form four subcommittees based on what matters to each of us the most? Cade, you're thinking about the vet. That's a service issue. Christy, you're worried about the parks and community center. Those are quality-of-life issues. I'm concerned about local businesses."

His insight was a relief. He saw the big picture in a way Erica didn't.

"We'll need four volunteers to head up the committees," Marc continued. "And the members will have tasks to complete before the club meets again. Research only. No decisions or actions will be made without a vote."

Erica looked around the room. A few people had the deer-in-headlights look. A few were nodding. And a few were staring at the table as if they wished they could disappear.

"Should we take a vote about the committees?" Erica asked.

"I like the idea," Christy said. "Anyone have a better one?"

Erica automatically turned her attention to Clem. For once, he had nothing to add. Another relief.

"Okay, we need four volunteers to head the committees." She doubted she'd get four hands, but who knew? Maybe she'd be surprised.

"I'll head up the service committee," Cade said as he raised his hand.

"And I'll head up the business committee," Marc said. Smiles and nods abounded.

"I'll be happy to be in charge of the quality-of-life committee," Erica said. "That is, if anyone else doesn't want it."

"You're a natural, Erica. It's all yours," Christy said with a kind smile. Then she turned to Clem. "And, Clem, I think you should be in charge of the miscellaneous. You've always been a jack-of-all-trades."

His chest seemed to puff up. "If I say yes, then everyone on my committee needs to pull their own weight. I don't take kindly to slackers."

Murmurs rippled around the table, and they took a vote. All were in favor.

"With that settled," Erica said, "each of you can join the committee you think would suit you best."

Gradually, everyone stood up and made their way to

either Cade, Marc, Clem or Erica. Clem had the fewest people on his committee—two—while the rest each had three volunteers. The one person who hadn't joined a committee was the older man with the blue eyes who had been last to speak.

Erica addressed the room. "Committee leaders will reach out to their groups to start researching the items we listed tonight. In the meantime, I'll email my notes to everyone. Thank you for coming. And thank you for working together on this. Together we can make Jewel River vibrant again."

When the meeting ended, people chatted and made their way to the door.

Erica took the opportunity to approach the mystery man. "Excuse me, but we haven't met. I'm Erica Black."

"Johnny." He thrust his hand out, and she shook it. His eyes brightened with cheer. "Johnny Abbot."

"I live out at Winston Ranch. My great-aunt and uncle owned it."

He nodded. "I knew them both. Fine people. I'm on Bear Creek Highway. It's a good spot for hunting and fishing."

"I'm sure." They spent a few minutes getting to know each other, and then Erica figured she might as well ask him to help. "Would you like to join a committee?"

"I'm not much of a joiner." He pushed his glasses up the bridge of his nose.

"That's okay. We all have our gifts. At least, that's what my mom tells me." She grinned. "Maybe that was just her way of being nice, though."

"I don't know that I have anything to offer."

"Everyone has something to offer." She patted his arm. "We're glad you're here. Please keep coming."

He shoved a stocking cap on his head, gave her a friendly nod and headed to the door. Erica realized only Cade and Christy were left. She wriggled her arms into her jacket and slung her purse over her shoulder as they waited for her near the entrance.

"Have I told you how glad I am you're doing this?" Christy wound her arm in Erica's. "I've been complaining about the deterioration of our town for years. And here you are taking charge and actually doing something about it. Thank you."

It had been a long time since Erica had felt appreciated. A long time.

"It's my pleasure." Erica put her other hand over Christy's. "Thank *you* for joining and helping."

"Wouldn't miss it. And don't worry about old Clem. He eats razor blades for breakfast. The man is cranky. Always in a bad mood."

"Well, he is heading up a committee," Erica said. "He can't be all bad."

"Oh, he's bad." Christy laughed.

They emerged into the parking lot as Cade locked the door to the community center behind them. A cold wind blew, and the black sky held no sign of the moon.

"I'm glad I'm on your committee." Christy let go of her arm. "I have oodles of ideas to make this town shine."

"Yes, Erica, I'm glad she's on your committee, too," Cade teased.

Christy lightly hit him in the chest. "Behave yourself." He chuckled.

They said goodbye, and Erica hurried to her truck. After getting in, she turned it on and let it warm up for a few minutes. Dalton was arriving tomorrow—much earlier than she'd expected—and knowing he'd be in charge of everything took a load off her mind. With the ranch taken care of, she could devote more time to the legacy club and to figuring out what to do with the pole barn.

Yes, Dalton accepting the job was a good thing. If she was wrong, she'd deal with it.

This was home. As Dalton pulled into Winston Ranch Wednesday afternoon, he was overcome with emotion. A new chapter in his life. Taking care of the cattle. Riding his horse every day. Going home to a spacious, private cabin. Earning enough money to have a life. A future. Sugarpie was in the trailer hitched to the truck, and he couldn't wait to get her unloaded.

He'd been able to move sooner than he'd expected. He'd talked to his boss at the feedstore on Monday, and the man had told him they had enough workers to cover his shifts. No need for him to give notice. Then Erica had given Dalton the all-clear to move in today.

It didn't get better than this. Well, except for the Erica factor. And then there was their exes. He couldn't forget he might be forced to interact with Jamie at some point in the future.

Dalton frowned. Why was he ruining the moment? He was going to enjoy the day. It had been a long time—years, in fact—since he'd felt this much hope.

Taking note of the surrounding pastures, he continued driving down the long, winding lane. The skies were bright with sunshine, but the air had grown cold and tiny snowflakes descended to the ground. He passed the main house and wondered if Erica was out and about. Then he continued on, driving to the outbuildings and the horse pasture.

It was time to get Sugarpie used to her new surroundings. Hopefully, Erica had done as he'd asked and prepared a paddock for Sugarpie, so she could get used to the other horses without being put together with them too soon.

He parked the truck near the stables and got out. Shivering under his unzipped coat, he strode toward the barn where the ranch office was located. A bow-legged man with stooped shoulders greeted him from the door.

"You must be Dalton Cambridge. Come in here." The man waved him in, and once inside, Dalton shook the man's hand. "Sonny Bay. Been running this ranch for purt' near fifty years. Wish I had more time to teach you everything, son, but this hip—" he slapped his left hip "—has it in for me. I never thought I'd say this, but I can't wait to have it replaced on Friday. Don't tell the missus. She would never let me hear the end of her I-told-you-so's."

Dalton followed him into the office and took a seat in a wooden chair, while Sonny eased himself into the desk chair and opened a file cabinet in search of something.

"Here's the schedule. Dewey and I wrote it all down years ago. We run a tight ship. You have any questions, you call me. And Lars, Braylen and Sam know their stuff. Got 'em trained right." The man handed him a binder. "You can read it all later. First, let's see this horse of yours and get her out to pasture."

Sonny got to his feet and limped out the office. They went through the barn and out the door, stopping behind the trailer.

"You see the paddock behind that shed?" Sonny pointed. Dalton nodded. "That's where you can put her. The rest of the horses are in the adjacent pasture and will likely come up and introduce themselves in no time. Is your girl skittish?"

"No, she's friendly and calm." Dalton began unlocking the back of the trailer.

"Good. Lead her over to the gate. I'll open it for you when you're ready." Sonny let out a low whistle when Dalton finished backing Sugarpie out of the trailer. "She is a beauty."

Over the next twenty minutes, Dalton moved the horse from the trailer to the paddock, then fed and watered her while giving her plenty of love. He stayed with her as she shook her mane and snorted, nudging him to keep petting her muzzle. He chuckled and obliged. In the distance, two horses sauntered their way.

"See? What did I tell you? The horses are like teens with a new kid in school—nosy as all get out. If you want to stay with her awhile, go ahead." Sonny handed him an envelope. "Here's the key to your cabin. Stop by the office first thing tomorrow morning, and I'll show you how we do things around here."

"Thanks, Sonny. I appreciate it."

The man grew serious. "I hate to leave it. The wife's been nagging me for years to retire, and I figure it's time. I'm glad Erica chose you and not some tenderfoot with no understanding of cattle ranching in this part of Wyoming."

"Well, my ranch was an hour and a half from here."

"Close enough. And it's my understanding you grew up ranching. That's the important thing."

A lump formed in his throat. It was important. It had been the most important thing in his life, besides Haley and Grady.

And he'd lost all three.

Well, not Grady. Dalton would have him this weekend. A few weeks ago, he'd worked out the pick-up time for

Friday evening. He winced. Haley had texted him several times about the preschool money. He needed to give her a check. He also needed to tell her he'd gotten a new job and moved. To Erica's ranch. That conversation would not go well.

"Is anyone meeting you here to help you unload?" Sonny led the way to the paddock gate, and after Dalton exited, he closed it properly.

"No."

"I'll send Lars over as soon as he's back from checking cattle."

"That's not necessary."

"I'm still the ranch manager. I'll be the judge of what's necessary. For one more day, at least. Lars will be over soon." Sonny tipped the brim of his hat to Dalton. "Now go on. I won't keep you any longer."

"Thanks, Sonny."

"You're welcome." The man winked and limped back toward the ranch office.

Dalton turned to check on Sugarpie. She'd made her way to the fence where the two horses were now standing. They all seemed to be getting to know each other. No signs of tension. He could rest easy.

With a spring in his step, he got back into the truck, drove down the lane and unhitched the trailer next to the other horse trailers, then looped back around the buildings and farther down the lane, where the cabins were located. He passed a charming one-story cottage with a Christmas wreath on the door. Must be the housekeeper's place. Then he continued down the gravel lane until he reached the final cabin, nestled among pine trees.

He backed up to the front porch. Then he hopped out, jogged up the porch steps and unlocked the front door.

The cabin sparkled. Smelled clean and fresh. A welcome basket sat on the kitchen counter. He plucked the card out with his name on it and opened it.

Dalton,
Welcome to Winston Ranch! I'm excited to have you on board as the new manager. Please let me know if you need anything. Sonny will show you around the ranch.
Enjoy your new home!
Erica

He traced her name, and the corners of his lips twitched into a smile. Then he examined the basket lined with a rust-colored cloth napkin. A package of ground coffee, a loaf of pumpkin bread, scissors, a pen, a pad of paper and a mug completed the gift. He raised the mug. Black with white lettering. Life is Better on the Ranch.

The gesture brought unexpected emotions to his throat, and he set down the mug. Clenched his jaw and breathed through his nose until he felt settled again.

Erica was thoughtful. He'd give her that.

Life is Better on the Ranch—yes. He wouldn't argue with that. And it was time to make this ranch his home.

Dalton poked into the rest of the rooms—all freshly vacuumed and cleaned—then went back out to the truck to unload his stuff. A buddy from work had helped him load it this morning. Hadn't taken long. He didn't have much. He lowered the tailgate and took a step back.

Maybe Sonny was right about having Lars come over. Dalton rubbed his chin as the cold started seeping into his bones. He'd unload the boxes first. Would give him time to figure out how to get the larger pieces out.

After unloading the fourth box, he did a double take.

"Thought I saw your truck here." Erica's smile was as bright as the noonday sun as she strode up the driveway. Her hands were in her coat pockets, and a stocking cap with a furry pompom covered the top of her head. The jeans she had on ended in winter boots.

Even in basic jeans and winter wear, this woman was a knockout. For the first time since arriving, he felt a twinge of anxiety.

"Does everything look okay in there?" she asked. "I cleaned it yesterday."

"It's great." His tongue stuck to the roof of his mouth like putty. "Thanks for the basket."

"You're welcome." Her dimples flashed, and he had to avert his eyes. "Want some help?"

"Um, that's okay." He didn't want her around. Not because he didn't like her, but because he did. "Sonny said Lars will come over."

She ignored him and moseyed to the back of the truck. He scooted away a few inches.

"Slide that bin my way." She pointed to a small blue bin.

"It's okay. Really. I've got this."

"Well, that wouldn't be very friendly of me." Her forehead wrinkled. "I'll help you unload. It's no trouble."

A couple of boxes. That's it. Then she'll leave.

"Hey, Erica!" a burly voice boomed from the end of the driveway. The cowboy in his midtwenties ambled their way. "Sonny said I should come over and help unload."

"It's a good thing, too. He doesn't think he needs help." Grinning, she jerked her thumb Dalton's way. They all stepped back to study the bed of his truck.

"If we get the nightstand and these boxes out of the

way," Dalton said to Lars, "we can deal with the bigger stuff."

"I'll work on the boxes," Erica said. Dalton handed her the blue bin she'd requested, and she carried it inside.

Within thirty minutes, the entire truck was unloaded, and Lars waved goodbye and whistled a tune on his way back to the stables, leaving Dalton and Erica alone.

"I can't wait for you to meet Gemma," Erica said as they went inside. She walked over to the kitchen counter and pointed at the basket. "She's the one who made the pumpkin bread. She's the best."

Dalton stood a few feet from her. Now that everything had been moved in, he wanted to be alone. But he couldn't exactly kick out his boss.

"She loves kids, too, and she's already asked about Grady. I hope you don't mind introducing him to her. She used to run a day care in her home, so kids and Gemma go together like peanut butter and jelly."

"She sounds great." He stretched his neck to the side to work out a kink. As easy as Erica was at making conversation, he just wanted this one to end. It had been a long day. And he'd picked up the scent of her perfume. Caught the glimmer in her eyes whenever those dimples appeared. Found himself tempted by her pretty face and easy personality all over again.

But she was his boss. And a key player in his post-divorce life. He couldn't go there.

"Well, I'll get out of your hair." She turned to leave and waved. "Have fun getting settled."

"Thanks." As soon as she was outside and off the porch, he shut the door. Then he went to the couch, collapsed on it and let his head fall back against the cushions.

Ready or not, he was officially working for Erica Black. And he had no idea if he could handle it.

"Are you ready to see Grady?" Erica pushed a large, plastic tractor Rowan's way Friday night a few minutes before seven. They were both on the floor of the living room. A bucket of toys had been dumped in the middle of the rug.

"Gwady!" Rowan threw his hands in the air. Erica chuckled and glanced up at Gemma, who was slowly rocking in the recliner as she flipped through the channels.

"How about you, Gemma? Are you ready?" When Erica told her this afternoon about inviting Dalton and his son over tonight to meet her, Gemma's response hadn't surprised her. The woman had wrung her hands and claimed she didn't want to intrude. Erica had assured her it wasn't an intrusion—it was an introduction. That way Gemma would feel comfortable if she ran into Dalton around the ranch. She shied away from being around anyone she didn't know well.

"Oh, I suppose," Gemma said, frowning.

Erica was used to Gemma raving about Rowan. She often spent five to ten minutes gushing over his latest achievement, no matter how small. The woman adored kids. Gemma was going to love little Grady. "I appreciate you staying to meet them."

Knock, knock.

After pushing herself to a kneeling position, Erica set one foot on the ground, then the other and winced as she made her way to the front door. Her muscles were tight.

She opened the door and grinned at the sight of Dalton in his cowboy hat holding his son on his hip.

"You made it. Come in, come in. It's cold out there."

She waved them inside and closed the door. After they took off their coats and boots, she gestured for them to follow her into the living room. She looked over her shoulder. "It's getting dark out earlier and earlier. I miss summer already."

"I do, too." Dalton held Grady's hand. The boy was supercute. He had blond hair and brown eyes like his daddy's. He was taller than Rowan; not surprising, since he was several months older. Rowan would be three next month, and Grady had turned three this summer.

"Hi there, Grady, I'm Miss Erica, Rowan's mommy."

Grady grabbed Dalton's jeans and hid his face behind his leg.

Erica chuckled. "Don't worry, I don't bite. Why don't you join us? We're playing with cars and tractors."

Gemma had gotten out of the chair and was standing there, wringing her hands. A sense of remorse washed over Erica. The past couple of years had been difficult for Gemma. The woman rarely left the ranch, preferring to be alone, or with Erica and Rowan.

"Gemma Redmond, I'd like you to meet the new ranch manager, Dalton Cambridge."

Dalton stepped forward, holding out his hand. "It's nice to meet you, ma'am."

Gemma hesitated, then her face flushed and she shook his hand, but didn't say a word.

"And this is Grady." Erica turned to the boy with a smile. "Rowan gets to hang out with Grady on the weekends he spends with his daddy."

"Gwady!" Rowan ran over and held up a monster truck. "Want a twuck?"

"It's okay. You can play." Dalton pried his son's fingers loose from his jeans. "I'm right here."

Erica met Dalton's gaze above the boy's head. He seemed embarrassed, but he didn't need to be. Rowan tended to hang back in new places, too.

"Well, I've been having so much fun with this tractor, I'm going to keep playing with it." She winked at the boys and folded her body back onto the carpet, already regretting when she'd have to haul herself back up. "My farm needs to be plowed."

Grady held the monster truck and stood there as if he needed permission to move. Rowan had plopped down on his tummy and was pushing a toy truck in a semicircle and making *vroom-vroom* sounds. She smiled and patted the carpet next to her. Grady came over and got on all fours, then moved the monster truck forward, crawling with it until it stopped near Rowan's.

Erica kept one eye on the boys and monitored the interaction between Gemma and Dalton. He'd taken a seat on the sectional. His legs were apart and he was resting his elbows on his knees as he made idle conversation with her housekeeper. Gemma, for her part, seemed to be slightly more relaxed. Progress.

"Erica mentioned you watch Rowan for her. It's a blessing, I'm sure."

"I love spending time with Rowie." She was sitting in the recliner. "How old did you say Grady is?"

"Three. His birthday was in July."

"He's darling. So tall." She gave the child a fond smile, and Erica let out a small sigh of relief. "It will be nice for them to be able to play together here, too. How wonderful." Gemma beamed.

"Uh, I don't think they'll be spending much time together here."

Erica pretended to push the tractor as she shamelessly

eavesdropped. Rowan didn't have any children to play with. It would be good for him to have a friend around now and then. Not the whole weekend, or anything...

"It might be fun for them to have regular playdates." Gemma shifted to give him her full attention.

He looked flustered. "My time is short with him. I only get to have him every other weekend. I try to make the most of our time together."

Gemma gave him an understanding smile. "Good for you. But if you change your mind, I'd be happy to watch them for an hour or two. See how well they play together?"

His gaze moved to the boys, and Erica's did, too. Grady was kneeling beside Rowan. They began to race the trucks, laughing all the while.

"Let's jump 'em!" Rowan scrambled to his feet, pulled a throw pillow off the couch and proceeded to drive his truck up the pillow and let it go. It didn't go far.

"We need a ramp." Grady looked around for something to use.

Rowan ran over to Erica and tugged on her shirt. "Mama, we need a wamp."

A ramp. Sure they did. She pictured toys flying through the air, hitting the television or the boys. But their eager, hopeful expressions got to her, and she decided she wouldn't mind helping them build a ramp. After all, her brothers had been rough-and-tumble, too, when she was a kid. And more often than not, she'd joined them in their escapades.

"I don't think that's a good idea," Dalton said. "We don't want to break anything."

Grady's chin dropped to his chest and the truck he was holding fell to the floor.

"I think we'll be okay if we put it in the middle here," Erica said, pointing to an open space.

Grady's chin popped back up, and his look of hope made her want to wrap him into a big hug.

She got up, her knees creaky, and dusted her hands off on her jeans. "Rowan, Grady, why don't you move the toys to the side, while I find something you can use for a ramp. If that's okay with you, Dalton?"

With an uneasy expression, he nodded. "Just for a few minutes, though. We've got to head back."

She gave him a quick glance but decided against responding. It had been nice of him to stop by and meet Gemma. He clearly treasured his time with Grady, and she didn't blame him. If she only had every other weekend with Rowan, it would break her heart.

The entertainment center was filled with board games and picture books, so she grabbed a stack of both.

"When the little ones are done playing, I made them frosted sugar cookies in the shape of turkeys," Gemma said. "Thanksgiving will be here before we know it."

Erica set the stack on the floor and glanced at her. "One of these days, I'm going to convince you to come to Sunrise Bend with me for Thanksgiving. You would love it. My mom and dad cook a huge meal. All my siblings and their families will be there. The one thing you wouldn't like is the nonstop football, though. No matter how many times we try to change the channel to a movie, football somehow gets turned back on."

"I appreciate the offer, but I'm fine right here." Gemma averted her eyes.

"What about you, Dalton?" Erica asked. "What are you doing for Thanksgiving?"

"Uhh…" He rubbed his neck.

She began stacking books to make the ramp. "Do you spend it with family?"

"My grandparents passed away years ago. They raised me. I'm not sure what I'm doing this year."

She wanted to kick herself. It sounded like he didn't have a family to fall back on. Hers might annoy her at times, but she was grateful to have them.

"Well, you can always come with me to Sunrise Bend. That goes for both of you." She pointed her finger to Dalton, then Gemma. "The more, the merrier."

Gemma shook her head with a warm smile and addressed Dalton. "I'll go package up those cookies for you to take with you."

"Or you can eat them here." Erica checked to see how the boys were faring as they launched their trucks from the ramp. So far, so good. "We have chocolate milk and everything."

Dalton flushed and gave a small shake of his head. "Chocolate milk is tempting, but Grady and I are going to head back. We'll stay five more minutes, okay, bud?"

"Okay, Daddy." Grady and Rowan were in the process of stacking more picture books on the pile to make the ramp higher.

"Oh, they're going to topple. Here, let's lean the books up against the games." Erica showed the boys how to lean them, taking off one of the board games in the process. "Too high. There. That's better. Now, point them in that direction, okay?" She nodded toward the open space that led to the kitchen island and stools.

The boys pushed their trucks up the ramp and, squealing with delight, ran after them again and again. Each time, the books would collapse, so Erica stayed close to fix the ramp.

"It's time to wrap it up, Grady. Let's help Rowan put the toys away." Dalton loomed over them. Erica hadn't noticed him get up.

"No, we're playing!" Grady's face said it all—he was having fun and didn't want to stop.

"It's been more than five minutes." His voice was firm. "Time to go."

The boy's lower lip jutted out, but he began gathering the toys, and Rowan dragged the basket over for them to fill. Soon, they made a game out of throwing everything into it. The giggling grew loud. It made Erica want to giggle, too. Little scamps.

"Are you sure you don't want to stay for chocolate milk and cookies?" She'd somehow gotten herself off the floor again and stood next to him, watching the boys.

"Not tonight. But thanks. This was, ahh…good. For Grady." He met her gaze then, and she wondered if she was imagining the words unspoken—*and for me, too.* Had it been good for him to come over? Or did he feel like it was half an hour of time with Grady he'd lost?

"All right. Well, I'll be seeing you Monday afternoon then. I'll stop by the ranch office, and we can discuss Sonny's checklist."

She gabbed with Dalton and Grady as they put their coats back on, then picked up Rowan, who was rubbing his tired eyes. Gemma bustled over with a covered paper plate full of beautifully decorated cookies, and everyone said their goodbyes.

Once they'd left, Erica turned to Gemma. "Well, what did you think?"

"I think he's a good daddy. And that little boy is darling. I hope Dalton changes his mind about Grady coming over to play with Rowie, though. You saw how much they enjoyed each other." Gemma opened the hall closet and took out her coat. She put it on and zipped it, then pulled gloves out of the pockets. Then she came closer and kissed Rowan on the cheek. "Good night, sweetheart."

"Wove you, Gwammy Gemma." He blew her kisses, and she laughed.

Erica set Rowan back on his feet and pointed him in the direction of his bedroom. "Go get your jammies on. Then we'll watch a cartoon."

Gemma reached for the door handle.

"Gemma? Did it bother you? Having him here?"

"Sometimes it's hard to meet new people, but he's nice."

"If it's too much—you know, being here with him around—let me know."

Gemma blinked rapidly as she smiled. "Thank you, Erica. It's not too much."

Erica gave her a quick hug, and she left.

Blowing out a long breath, she padded down the hall to Rowan's room. She was glad Gemma liked Dalton. And she was glad it wasn't too much for the woman to be around him. Surprisingly, having Dalton here with his son wasn't too much for her, either.

But maybe it should be. It was all fun and games until their exes got involved.

Their exes. Erica hadn't told Jamie about hiring Dalton yet. She'd have to do it soon. It wouldn't go well. She already knew it. But she also knew it really didn't matter what her ex thought of her new manager.

The ranch was her home now. It was Rowan's future. And Dalton would make sure it was run well. She was certain of it.

Chapter Five

He'd been dreading this moment all weekend. Late Sunday afternoon, Dalton knocked on the front door of the sprawling two-story home Haley shared with Jamie. He needed to tell Haley that he'd moved and that he was working for Erica.

He probably should have mentioned it on Friday, but it would have put a damper on his time with Grady, and he'd figured waiting until today wouldn't hurt anyone. Yesterday, Dalton had taken Grady for a long ride with him on Sugarpie, and this morning they'd made pancakes after church. It had been the best weekend he'd had in years.

Next summer, he'd start teaching Grady to ride a horse on his own. At some point he'd have to buy a small horse for the boy. It was an expense that would have to wait until he saved some money, though. Maybe Erica planned on buying one for Rowan. If she did, she might let him pay her to let Grady use it for lessons.

The door opened, and he shoved aside all the horse thoughts. Haley appeared as beautiful and fragile-looking as ever. Seeing her always tugged at his emotions. He'd wrapped all of his future dreams around her. And she'd taken them all away from him.

"There you are." She held her arms out to Grady, who ran into them and hugged her. "Well, this is a nice welcome." With a loving expression, she caressed his hair. Dalton would give her that—she loved their son.

"Hey, Grady, I'll see you soon, okay?" Dalton crouched to give the boy a hug. Then he kissed the top of his head. "I love you."

"I love you, too, Daddy!" Grady dropped his backpack on the floor in the foyer and ran down the hall, out of sight.

"Can I talk to you for a minute?" Dalton shifted his weight to one hip.

"Sure, come in."

"No. Alone." He didn't budge. There was no way he was walking into their house and being bombarded with her perfect new life.

She shivered under her expensive sweater set. "It's too cold to talk on the porch."

"Fine." He took one step into the foyer and closed the door. "We can talk here."

Her eyes widened as if to say *whatever*. Her blond hair was smoothed into a low ponytail, and she had on diamond earrings. A gift from her husband, no doubt. Annoyed with himself for even thinking about her and her stupid earrings, he brought his attention back to the task at hand.

"I moved," he said. "Took a new job."

"Oh?" She looked taken aback. "Where?"

"Jewel River."

"But that's where—"

"I'm managing Winston Ranch." There. He'd said it. Better to get it out now. It wasn't as if he could keep it a secret. Not with their drop-off and pick-up arrangement.

"Winston Ranch?" Her blue eyes flashed with anger as her face went slack. "Erica's ranch? Jamie's ex-wife?"

"Yes." He tightened his jaw, refusing to feel guilty.

"Jamie," she called over her shoulder. "Could you come here?"

"I didn't agree to this. I said I'd talk to you alone." Dalton held out his palms and backed up a step. "You know how I feel about him."

"It affects him, too." She lifted her chin.

"What's up, babe?" As soon as Jamie appeared, Dalton curled his fingers into his palms. The guy was tall, good-looking and wore expensive athletic clothes. Made him feel like a country bumpkin in comparison.

"Did you know that Dalton's managing Erica's ranch?" Each word was an accusation.

"What?" Jamie went from easygoing to flaming hot in a split second. "Is this some kind of joke?"

"I can't believe you're being this childish, Dalton." Haley glared at him as she shook her head in disappointment.

Anger spiked his adrenaline. Childish? Getting a good-paying job—one that made him happy—and having a chance at a decent life was childish?

"What's this about? Is she trying to get even with me or something?" Jamie barked out a sarcastic laugh. "I hate to tell you, but the joke's on you for working for Erica. You'll see."

It was on the tip of his tongue to tell him off, but Haley spoke before he could. "We'll discuss this more after I've had a chance to process it. For now, I need that preschool check. If you'd get with this century, you could download the app and transfer me the money."

Preschool check. This century. Transfer the money.

She might as well have put him in the corner for a time-out, the way she did with Grady.

Is that how his ex-wife saw him? As a child? Someone too stupid and immature to handle life?

This wasn't new. Hadn't she always made him feel inferior? It had been a staple of their relationship. He'd been too in love with her to recognize it.

Dalton took the folded check out of his pocket and handed it to her. He gave Jamie the briefest of glances—the guy made a show of putting his arm around Haley's shoulders—and pivoted on his heel, letting himself out.

He was tired of feeling less-than. And every time he saw his ex-wife or her husband, that's how he felt. Like they considered him beneath them. Because they did.

"This isn't over, Dalton," Haley said.

For him, it was. As he descended their porch steps, he made himself a promise. He was never, ever stepping foot in that house again.

He wasn't beneath them. And he was tired of being treated like he was.

Erica inhaled the crisp winter air as she strolled down the driveway past the stables to the ranch office on Monday afternoon. It had been a good weekend. She'd contacted the three members of her committee, and after some heavy persuasion, had gotten them all to agree on the calls they needed to make before the legacy club meeting next month.

After church yesterday, Clem had cornered her to complain about Angela Zane and her over-the-top ideas for designing a town flag. While she personally agreed with Clem that a town flag was the least of their worries at this point, she knew Angela had a big, generous heart, and she'd told him so. He'd made a sucking sound with his teeth, pointed to her and said, "Then take her on *your* committee, missy."

The problem was she already had Mary Corning—who was brimming with grand plans—and Christy Moulten, and Erica didn't think she could handle Angela, too. She'd told Clem they could trade. He'd considered for a moment and shook his head, then stalked away without another word.

She didn't need to think about any of that now. It was a beautiful, cold day, and she couldn't wait to check in with Dalton to find out what he thought about the ranch. Today was his first official day as the manager. Thankfully, Sonny's hip surgery had gone well on Friday. Erica had sent flowers to the hospital and talked to his wife, who'd sounded excited for him to heal so they could travel together.

The open bay of the barn beckoned, and she strolled inside, noting how orderly it appeared, and headed to the back corner, where the ranch office was located. She paused in the doorway. Dalton was sitting at the desk, poring over a ledger.

"Mind if I come in?" She flashed him a smile, wanting this meeting to go well. She wasn't sure how their professional relationship would work, and it seemed important to get it off on the right note.

His head popped up, and he waved her inside. "Sure, take a seat."

"How did your first day go?" Erica pulled out the wooden chair and sat, crossing one leg over the other.

"Fine." He set down his pen and stretched with his hands at the back of his head. He looked tired. And unhappy.

Was he unhappy here? Already? She'd thought this was the perfect solution to both of their problems. She'd get a ranch manager, and he'd get a ranch to run. What if she was wrong?

"Are the other cowboys respecting you?" Maybe they were the problem. She wouldn't tolerate it if they were.

"Yes. They know what they're doing. I hardly have to say a word and they're on it."

Okay, so they weren't the problem.

"Anything going on that I should be aware of?"

"Why do you ask?" His eyes flashed with leeriness.

"No reason." She shrugged and picked at her fingernail. "You just seem…off."

"I guess you already know." He met her gaze then, and her stomach soured at the war zone in his expression. What did she already know? Nothing came to mind. She braced herself for bad news. He sighed. "Yesterday, when I dropped off Grady, I told Haley about moving here and working for you."

"Oh." That's why she'd gotten several texts, a missed call and a voice mail from Jamie last night. She'd ignored them all. She was used to him harassing her over the most minor of details.

"She's not happy about it. Your ex isn't, either."

"I see." Her mouth grew parched. She swallowed, waiting for him to explain further. But he didn't. "What about you?"

"What about me?"

"Are you happy working here?"

A whisper of a smile appeared on his lips. "Yes, I am."

"Then that's all that matters." She hitched her chin up. Case closed.

"It's not that easy."

"Why not?" she asked. "They're happy. Aren't you allowed to be, too?"

He propped an elbow on the desk and let his temple rest against two fingers. Then he shook his head slightly. He looked defeated, and it made her mad. Her ex always got his way. Even in this.

"Dalton, I don't know what your relationship with Haley is like, but I know Jamie. He says one word and expects everyone to obey, whether his request is logical or not." She inwardly squirmed at all the ways she'd tried to make him happy, even when he was being ridiculous. "I should have told him first. Then you wouldn't have had to deal with him yesterday. I'm sorry."

He snapped to attention. "It's not your fault. I wasn't blaming you."

His words clicked something in her brain. "You're right. It isn't my fault. And it isn't yours, either. We have nothing to be blamed for. If anyone should feel guilty, it should be Jamie for cheating on me. Same goes for Haley and you."

She shut her mouth, unsure of how he'd react to criticism of his ex-wife.

"I know you're right." He stared unseeingly at the office door. "But this? I don't know. I think she might have a right to be mad."

"She lost that right when she asked you for a divorce." Erica wasn't holding back. Not on this topic. "It's none of her business where you live, where you work or what you do for a living as long as it doesn't hurt Grady."

He didn't look convinced.

"Would she ask for your permission to move to a new town? Or to work for someone who made you uncomfortable?"

"No."

Erica was under no illusions. When she was pregnant, all of Jamie's business trips had been spent with Haley, who'd been working for him in sales at the time. To this day, it gave her acid reflux.

Silence stretched as sounds of the ranch continued outside—a horse neighing in the distance, the wind rattling the barn's walls, the rumble of a UTV's engine as it drove by.

"It feels like I'll never be free of it," Dalton said.

"Free of what?"

"Her. Him."

"I know." She sighed. "I'm still trying to figure out who I am. I'm not the girl I was before I met Jamie, but I'm not sure who this new version of me is, either. I don't want to make the same mistakes."

Why had she told him all that? She hadn't even told her own mother those things.

"And I'm afraid I *am* the same guy. I don't even know what mistakes I made that I need to avoid."

Erica rubbed her empty ring finger. "You're a guy who got blindsided by his unfaithful wife. Same as me. Well, except for the wife part. Switch wife to husband, and you know what I mean."

He let out a snort.

"Jamie and Haley got what they wanted," Erica said. "They're living their happily-ever-after. If you working here makes them uncomfortable, too bad. They can't dictate to you or to me anymore. Not about this."

He gave her a wary look. "You didn't hire me for payback, did you? I don't want to be in the middle of some kind of revenge game."

"You know better than that." Was it true, though? For

a good six months after the divorce was final, Erica had wasted too much time fantasizing about ways to get Jamie back for ruining her life. But with the Good Lord's help, she'd turned her focus to herself and gradually stopped thinking about him. Sure, she still got an upsetting adrenaline rush when they argued, but it didn't mean she was playing games.

At some point, she hoped seeing Jamie wouldn't trigger any feelings at all. That she'd be able to stay calm when he pushed her buttons. Until then, she'd keep trying to move on. And she was trying.

"I don't need attention from my ex. I also don't need him weighing in on what's best for me or this ranch. I was honest with you. I hired you as a last resort. You know I did. And it's working out. I'm glad you're here. That doesn't make me the villain."

"I didn't… That is… You don't think I'm casting you as a villain in all this, do you?" For the first time today, he looked curious instead of downtrodden.

"No, I don't." She didn't, either.

"Good, because I do appreciate this opportunity. The ranch is great. Runs better than a new truck driving off the lot. Your cattle are healthy. Pastures seem to be well-rotated. Even the buildings are solid and most don't need repairs."

"Great. Now let's put our exes behind us." She pulled back her shoulders, happy to move on to more important subjects. "Lead me through the checklist."

For the next thirty minutes, Dalton gave her his opinion on each item on the list. Erica and Sonny had been reviewing the same general list together every weekday since she'd inherited the ranch.

When Dalton finished discussing the last item, they both stood.

"I meant it when I said I want you to let me know if you have any ideas on how to improve the ranch." She left the office with him on her heels.

"I will." They strode through the bay to the door that led outside.

"Lars and Sam are taking care of the cattle Thanksgiving weekend." Out in the cold, she shivered. "You can take all four days off. Will you have Grady?"

"No, I won't. Are you going home now?"

"I think I'll check on Murphy first."

"I'll join you." They continued down the lane toward the horse pasture.

"The offer still stands if you want to come to my family's ranch up in Sunrise Bend for Thanksgiving dinner." Her mom loved when extra people showed up for the holidays. And Dad and her brothers would like Dalton. Erica couldn't wait to catch up with Reagan and her sisters-in-law, Sienna and Holly. "I'll have Rowan. Jamie didn't put up a fight about it for once."

"Strange, isn't it?" he asked. The cold air kept her pace brisk.

"What's strange?"

"Haley wants Grady with them, but Jamie's letting Rowan stay with you?"

It was strange, now that she thought about it. Their custody arrangement tended to result in the boys being with Jamie and Haley on the same weekends, most likely so they could have the other weekends on their own without kids.

Which was another thing that irritated her.

"Yeah, well, I don't pretend to understand what goes

through my ex's head." Erica gave him a skeptical glance. "He probably didn't realize Haley has Grady. And when he does, he'll expect me to hand our son over. Not happening."

He laughed, and the cheerful sound was so unexpected, she stopped in her tracks and faced him.

"Do that again."

"Do what?" He frowned.

"Laugh." Grinning, she poked his chest. "You have a great laugh, Dalton."

His eyes shimmered, and what she saw in them made her wonder… Could Dalton be attracted to her? She certainly found him attractive.

The thought bothered her. She'd spent too much time with the cowboy today. Murphy would have to wait. "Uh, I forgot about something. I have to head back. I'll see you tomorrow."

"See you tomorrow." He lifted his finger in a semi-salute.

And all the way back to the house, she couldn't help thinking that Dalton was easy to be with. A nice guy. Too bad their situation made it impossible for her to think of him as an available man.

She had no intention of dating anyone right now, least of all her new ranch manager. And she'd certainly never consider dating Haley's ex. The woman was her exact opposite.

Erica hadn't been enough for Jamie, and she wouldn't be enough for Dalton, either. She'd better not forget it.

"Oh, thank you for coming." On Friday evening, Gemma opened the door to her cabin wide, smiled and ushered Dalton inside. After reviewing the checklist with Erica, Dalton had gone home to shower, changed into clean clothes and had been towel-drying his hair when Gemma texted him, asking if he could help her with some boxes.

Wasn't like he had any other Friday-night plans. Haley had Grady this weekend, leaving him with free time he didn't know what to do with.

"I hated to ask you to come over, Daltie, but the decorations are too heavy for me to get out this year."

Daltie? That was a new one.

"I don't mind, Gemma." He truly didn't mind helping her. She'd had Erica give him baked goods more than once this week, and her sweet nature made him overlook the nickname. He gave her a big smile. "If you'll point me in the right direction…"

As he followed her down the hall, the aroma of something delicious wafted to him. Something Italian. Spaghetti? His stomach growled, and he placed his hand against his abdomen, willing it to calm down.

"Here we are." She entered a large utility room at the back of her cabin and opened a door leading to a walk-in closet. "The tree is on the floor, but it's heavy, and everything else is in boxes up there."

The closet was crammed with…everything. Cardboard boxes, plastic bins and miscellaneous items. Locating the box with her artificial tree, he grabbed hold of it with both hands and hauled it out. "Where do you want this?"

"In the living room. By the front window. I like to see the lights shining through when I come home from taking care of Rowie."

He took it to the living room, then returned to the closet for the rest of the stuff. Gemma proceeded to point out the bins and boxes she needed. When he had them all moved to the living room, he asked her if she needed help putting the tree together.

"Oh, no. I couldn't ask you to do that." Her eyelashes fluttered as she dropped her gaze.

"I don't mind. Really." The Italian aroma hit him again. There had to be garlic bread in there, too. His mouth watered at the delicious smells.

"Well, it's three pieces. If you can assemble it, I'll be okay fluffing it."

"You sure?"

She nodded with bright, happy eyes.

"Okay." It took him less than ten minutes to assemble the tree. He plugged it in, and the colorful lights brought good memories to mind. Christmas had always been his favorite time of the year.

"Thank you." She stood back, clasping her hands, her expression full of joy. "Now, I have one more favor to ask."

He hoped it wasn't time-consuming, because the food he was smelling was making him ravenous.

"Would you mind dropping off this lasagna to Erica? She doesn't have Rowie this weekend, and Friday nights are hard on her."

"Oh." He was taken aback. He hadn't thought much about Erica's personal life beyond their complicated divorce situations. He'd been thinking about her a lot over the week, though. She was complex, yet simple and easy to read. "Sure. I'll head over there now."

"Thank you." She went to the kitchen and came back shortly with a large tote bag dangling from her wrist and both hands holding a foil-covered casserole dish. "The cookies in the bag are for you."

"Well, thank you." While he enjoyed her cookies, he'd

wrestle a moose to the ground for a bite of that lasagna. "Text me if you need any more help, okay?"

"I will."

He put on his boots and coat, took the tote bag and casserole from her and, after she opened the door, stepped onto her porch.

"Oh, and, Daltie?"

"Yes?" he said, pausing.

"Erica is special. I don't know how much she's told you about how I came to live here, but Martha—her great-aunt—saved my life. And when Erica arrived with Rowan, I finally had something to live for. She means the whole world to me."

He didn't know what to say.

"Don't let her strength fool you," Gemma said. "She wears her heart on her sleeve. And that heart of hers is awfully big."

He wasn't sure what to make of that, so he tipped his hat to her and continued on his way.

Erica was strong. And smart. And treated him like her equal instead of her employee.

And she was entwined in his uncomfortable relationship with Haley. Bound to a lifetime of interaction with her ex as much as he was with his.

He wasn't here for a personal relationship with her. He worked for her. That was it.

And he liked working here more each day. Sugarpie had settled right in, too. The horse seemed to have an extra spring in her step now that they were together again.

When he reached the end of the driveway, he turned to take the path to the main house. The wind hit him in the face. The cold air was sharp. He hoped it wouldn't storm. High winds tended to destroy sections of the fencing. Seemed no matter how big or small a ranch was, repairing fence was a continuous chore.

His thoughts returned to Gemma. He should have asked her what she'd meant about Martha saving her life. But it wasn't his business. Her take on Erica had him curious, too. He'd been wary of Erica's intentions on hiring him from the second she'd stepped foot in the feedstore. He didn't miss that place one bit. But she'd been honest with him, and he believed her.

Haley had called him yesterday. She'd used her whisper voice to tell him how hurt she was that he was working for Erica and hadn't consulted her about it. Then she'd listed several concerns about the situation—none of them made sense to him—and stated he needed to quit.

In the past, her whisper voice, along with reasons and declarations that he needed to do something she wanted, would have made him spring into action, but this time, he didn't. All he could picture while his ex-wife droned on and on was Erica's compassionate face on Monday, when she'd said he didn't need to feel guilty. That he deserved to be happy.

When Haley had finally ended the call, he'd realized it was the first time in years that he'd felt good about himself after talking to her. And that included when they were married. Maybe he really was getting over her.

Dalton reached the walkway to Erica's house and bounded up the porch steps before knocking on her door. After a few minutes, the door opened and Erica appeared. Her eyes widened. "What are you doing here?"

"Gemma asked me to bring this over." He held up the casserole dish. "She needed help getting her Christmas decorations out."

"And you helped." Her eyes sparkled in delight. "Just what she needed. A strong man."

The compliment warmed him. "Yeah, well, the lasagna is for you. The cookies are for me."

"I might fight you for those cookies." She leaned her shoulder against the door frame.

"I might fight back." He couldn't help smiling. When was the last time he'd interacted with a woman like this? Playfully? Teasingly?

Never.

Erica straightened and rubbed her forearms. "Have you eaten yet?"

"No."

"Why don't you come in and have some of this lasagna?"

"Oh, I don't know." His stomach growled louder than a bear.

"If you have plans—"

"I don't."

"Then help me make a dent in this. There's no way I could eat an entire lasagna by myself in the next couple of days."

He shouldn't share a meal with her. He should pop a frozen pizza in the oven and watch old movies back at his cabin. But there was something pulling him forward, and it wasn't just the lasagna.

He found himself taking a step closer. "You talked me into it."

"Good. Now I don't have to eat alone." She retreated so he could enter.

Yeah, and now he didn't have to eat alone, either.

Chapter Six

Erica finished the last bite of her lasagna as Dalton explained how he intended to make the ranch's small feedlot more profitable. She enjoyed watching him talk shop. He looked younger, happier and more engaged than when they'd first met. It was obvious he was meant to be a rancher.

Which made her wonder what she was meant to do with her life. The pole barn held the key to the answer. If she could figure out a business to run in it, she'd feel like she had direction. That she wasn't being blown about like dead leaves in autumn.

An hour ago, she'd gotten off the phone with Reagan, and for the first time in her life, Erica had actually envied her sister. Reagan had sounded so animated as she described the process of making chocolates. Even more animated than she'd been when she started making candles with their mom several years ago. It still surprised Erica that Reagan had decided to walk away from their very successful company to learn how to make chocolates. Thankfully, Holly and Sienna—their sisters-in-law— had joined the business and loved working with Mom.

When would Erica find a career that she loved, too?

"I wanted to ask you," Dalton began as he selected another hunk of garlic bread, "when are you planning on teaching Rowan to ride a horse?"

The topic caught her by surprise. "Oh." She sat back slightly, frowning. "I don't know."

"Well, I'm getting Grady used to the saddle so he'll be able to learn next summer. But Sugarpie is too big for him to ride on his own. I might start looking for a small horse in the spring."

"I see your point." She still thought of Rowan as a baby, but he would be three at the end of December. And she and her siblings had all learned to ride before they were old enough to go to school. While she loved riding Murphy, she didn't have any desire to shop for a horse. That's where her brothers and father came in handy. They lived for that sort of thing. "I'll mention it to my dad at Thanksgiving. He'll know exactly where to look for a small horse, gentle and obedient, for the boys to learn how to ride."

She pictured Rowan and Grady taking turns riding a horse in the paddock, and it made her smile.

"I can't afford one at the moment. But in a few months…"

"Leave it to me. I'll have my dad start shopping for one." She waved in dismissal. "And if you want to wait to buy your own, Grady can borrow it for lessons."

"I could pay you to rent it—"

"No—oh, no." She shook her head. "I don't expect you to pay me. Whenever Grady is here, you can teach him with it."

"I don't expect freebies." The furrows in his forehead gave him a serious air.

"I know." She rested her back against the chair. "What if we made a deal? I'll get the horse. You teach the boys how to ride. You can teach Grady next summer, and then when Rowan is a little older, you can teach him, too."

It hit her that she was talking about long-term plans. Here. On the ranch. With Dalton.

"You've got yourself a deal." He grinned.

"Can I ask you something?"

He set his napkin next to the plate and nodded.

"Do you see yourself here in a year? Two? Longer?"

His jaw shifted. She blinked as she waited for him to respond.

"Um, yeah. I can see myself here, depending…" He had a caged look in his eyes. "I mean, I've only been here a short while, but it's a well-run ranch. My cabin's great, and Sugarpie's loving her new home. But I'm not going to lie and tell you I'll stay if Haley and Jamie make things uncomfortable. I don't want a repeat of last Sunday."

She kept forgetting the reason she'd had to talk him into the job in the first place. Their exes.

"I hear you. I can barely be in the same room as Jamie, let alone Haley. The two of them together?" She shivered, wincing. They brought out her petty, mean side. Erica didn't need to feel worse about herself than she already did.

He finished his second helping of lasagna, eyed the casserole dish for a third and pushed away the plate. The gesture felt familiar. Her brothers did the same thing.

"You remind me of my brothers." She tilted her head.

"How many do you have?"

"Two. I had three, but Cody died several years ago in a car accident."

"I'm sorry to hear that. Were you close?"

The pinch in her heart was familiar but grew less intense as time wore on. Cody's death had been especially hard since he'd been estranged from the family the year prior to the accident.

"He was the baby of the family, and I bossed him around, but boy, oh, boy, I loved him. My little sister, Reagan, was the closest to him. I still miss him. Still wish I would have done things differently the year before he died."

"Why do you say that?" Dalton stood and began stacking his silverware on the plate. Then he went into the kitchen. Erica did the same.

"Everyone in our family had a big falling-out with him. He'd made some poor choices that affected us all. We went the tough-love route and ended up getting cut off from him." A lump formed in her throat at the memory. She'd made her peace with it long ago, but it still hurt. "He did end up getting his life together before the accident. It's hard, though. I didn't try to reconcile with him, and I should have."

"I'm sorry." He set the plate in the sink and took hers out of her hand to put in the sink, too.

"Thanks. Every time I start feeling guilty, I remind myself that God's already forgiven me. I can move on. But sometimes I still wrestle with regrets, you know?"

"It is hard, and I do know." He had his serious face on, and they were standing close—close enough for her to reach up and trail a finger down his cheek, but she kept her hands to herself.

"What about you? Brothers? Sisters?" She turned to go back to the table.

"One brother. He's younger than me. He enlisted right out of high school. Currently lives in Texas."

"Are you close?"

"Not really. My grandparents raised us. Our mom was

in high school when she had me, and the following year she had Dax. She was in and out of our lives for a few years—I don't remember her—and finally gave custody to my grandparents."

No father. A mother who abandoned him and his brother. The complete opposite of her happy childhood. She picked up the casserole dish to take it to the kitchen.

"And your grandparents have since passed, right?" She looked back at him. He had the plate with the remaining garlic bread in one hand and the salt and pepper shakers in the other.

"Correct."

"That's hard. I'm sorry. I know I take my family for granted, but hearing that you've lost yours…well, I *really* take them for granted."

"Why do you say that?"

"I don't know. I feel this push-pull thing, and I have for years." Erica didn't normally share any of this, but Dalton was easy to talk to, and Gemma's lasagna must have loosened her tongue. She set the dish on the counter, then bent to find the plastic wrap. "Mom's always giving me advice, but I get salty and do what I want. Which disappoints her. And then she always ends up being right, and that annoys me. And on we go."

She ripped the plastic wrap off the roll with too much force. And, as usual, it curled within itself. Now she had to unravel it. Ugh.

Dalton chuckled, and she gave him a sharp glance. He clamped his mouth shut, eyes twinkling, then turned on the faucet and opened the cupboard below the sink. He found the dish soap and gave it a squirt into the sink.

"What are you doing?" She tossed the wadded plastic wrap onto the counter. It wasn't worth unraveling. She'd use foil.

"Washing dishes. Why?"

She wanted to look over both shoulders for a hidden camera. Her ex *never* did dishes. The sight of this strapping cowboy sudsing it up in the sink was making her pulse race.

"Um, no reason. Carry on." Erica took the aluminum foil out of the drawer and carefully tore off a new section. Then she covered the leftover lasagna and popped it in the fridge.

Working together in the kitchen—doing domestic things—made her aware of Dalton in a way she was trying hard not to be. As a man. An extremely appealing man. Inside and out.

Yes, he was her ranch manager. Yes, he was the ex of her ex's new wife.

But he was also a single, hunky cowboy.

And she was a single mom who hadn't thought of a man romantically in years—not since meeting Jamie—and it was hard not to notice Dalton.

They could be friends. That was safe. Anything more? Too dangerous.

She took a clean dishcloth and dipped it in the soapy water, then wrung it out and strode to the table. What would her mother say if she could see her now? Well, Mom would likely be ecstatic to think of Erica showing interest in a rancher. The woman had been determined to pair her and Reagan off with *nice cowboys* their entire lives.

Yes, her mom would love Dalton.

Erica finished wiping off the table and was on her way back to the kitchen when her cell phone rang.

"Heads up." She tossed the dishcloth in the direction of the sink. Dalton caught it and gave her a cockeyed smile. She lunged for her phone and answered it.

"Oh, good, I caught you," Christy Moulten said. She had a feeling this wasn't a courtesy call. "I just found out the roof collapsed at the community center."

"What? Why?" The ramifications trickled in. The residents of Jewel River used the community center for everything—meetings, family reunions, small wedding receptions. This didn't bode well.

"Water damage and old age. It's bad."

"How bad? A patch job? Or worse?"

"Worse. Larry Fritz called JJ Construction, and they said the structural damage goes beyond the roof. It will be unusable for several months."

"Oh, no."

"The Christmas bake sale is coming up next month, and we're going to have to find it a new home. Quickly."

"Yeah, the bake sale is a big deal. I'll see what I can come up with." They talked for a few more minutes before ending the call.

Erica looked back at Dalton, who'd finished washing the dishes. He folded the dish towel and hung it over the stove's handle.

"Everything all right?" he asked.

Setting her phone on the counter, she shook her head. "No. The community center's roof collapsed. There's structural damage. The center won't be usable for months."

He pointed to the archway. "Come on, let's talk about it in the other room."

She led the way to the living room and sat on the sectional, pulling one knee to her chest to face him. He sat on the other end.

"The Christmas bake sale is next month." She thought about all the possible places downtown where they could move it. If it was just a bake sale, they could probably have it in the church's all-purpose room. But the room wasn't big enough to host the bake sale and the accompanying bazaar. Local crafters had been working for months on their Christmas items. It wouldn't be fair to exclude them due to a lack of space. "It's more than a bake sale. It's a bazaar, too. The whole town comes out to support it."

"Can they move the event to another building?"

"None are big enough." She bit her lower lip, trying to think of a solution.

"They could split it up. The bake sale in one spot and the bazaar in another."

"They could." But she didn't like the idea. Two locations would mean less crossover sales. "It's better for everyone involved—including the people who are coming to it—if both are in the same spot."

He nodded. A few seconds ticked by. Then he opened his hands. "What about here?"

"What about here?" Her living room was big, but not *that* big.

"The pole barn."

The pole barn. *Duh.* Why hadn't she thought of that?

"Of course! It's a huge empty space. Perfect." They'd have the bake sale here, and all the vendors would have plenty of room to sell their items. As the idea marinated, the cons started coming to mind. "I don't know. The ranch is a good twenty minutes out of town. Would people show up?"

"They'll drive. It's not that far."

"What about tables and chairs?"

"Use the community center's chairs and tables."

"I wouldn't know where to begin. The event is always so festive, and I don't know that the barn would do it justice." She was making excuses, and she shouldn't be.

Hosting the annual bake sale sounded amazing, but it also scared her.

"What's wrong?" he asked. "I thought you were trying to find a use for the pole barn."

"I am." She nodded quickly. "But, well, I'm nervous."

"You?" he scoffed. "Come on."

"Yes, me."

"Why? I've never met anyone who gets things done the way you do. You think of something, and a second later you're in motion making it happen."

The compliment warmed her. "Yes, but that's stuff that has to get done."

"And this isn't?" he asked. "Host it here. If you need help getting it ready, I'm your man."

She blinked rapidly, his offer was so unexpected. She was used to doing things on her own, taking charge, because no one else stepped up. Certainly not Jamie. And here Dalton was. Stepping up. To help her. And he was under no obligation to help. Yet, he'd offered regardless.

"Okay." Erica nodded, getting excited all over again. "I'll call Christy and offer to host the bake sale in the pole barn."

"Right now?"

"I might as well." She was already off the sectional. "Before I talk myself out of it."

"You're sure?"

"You're right. I have this huge barn sitting there, and the community needs it. I'll call her now."

* * *

Well, he couldn't get out of helping her now.

Wednesday afternoon, Dalton pocketed his phone and pulled his glove back on before patting Sugarpie's neck and clicking his tongue for her to head home.

Home. Funny, how in a few weeks this place already felt like home.

Erica, brimming with excitement, had just called to let him know the bake sale organizers had reviewed their options and decided the ranch's pole barn was the ideal location for this year's event. And it tickled him pink that she hadn't been able to wait half an hour until their daily meeting to tell him. She'd called him immediately.

Since he'd offered to help set up the pole barn for the event, it looked like he'd be spending the next couple of weeks getting the place ready. With Erica.

It both excited him and made him nervous. Where Haley seemed to be disappointed in him constantly, Erica enthusiastically welcomed his ideas. She made him feel competent and smart.

How long would it be before he disappointed her, too?

Tucking his chin in his scarf, he tried to protect his face from the bitter cold. It had a been a long day of checking cattle and repairing a section of fence with Braylen while the other hands did assorted chores around the place. One of the tractors needed a new part, and two of the pregnant cows were on his watch list—they weren't gaining enough weight—but other than that, all was well.

Sugarpie knew the way home at this point. As soon as they reached the main trail, she picked up her pace. His phone rang again. His heart started tap-dancing. He liked hearing Erica's peppy voice. She'd probably thought up five more suggestions for the event. And he couldn't wait to hear all five of them.

Slowing Sugarpie, he took off his glove again and answered the phone. And wished he'd ignored it.

"Hi, Dalton," Haley said. "I have a favor to ask."

Here we go. More money. He tightened the grip on his phone. "Now's not a good time."

"Would you take Grady for Thanksgiving?"

Well, that wasn't what he'd been expecting. Thanksgiving was tomorrow. Erica had invited him several times to go to her parents' house, but he kept declining. He had no plans. His chest expanded as he thought about having his son all day tomorrow. "Of course, I'll take him."

"Oh, good!" Her breathy sigh of relief made him want to roll his eyes. "Jamie surprised me with a trip to Salt Lake City to do some Christmas shopping. We'll be back Sunday afternoon."

"I thought you said Thanksgiving." His tone hardened. While he'd love to spend the entire weekend with his son, it annoyed him that she assumed he'd have all four days free on such short notice.

"I meant Thanksgiving weekend..." Her voice trailed off. "If you can't watch him, I guess I'll have to see if Jamie's mom—"

"No. I'll watch him." Like he'd ever let that guy's mother watch his son when Dalton only wanted *more* time with the boy. No way.

"Are you sure?"

"Yes." He ground his teeth together. *Don't tell her off. It's not worth it. You're getting your son—that's the important thing.*

"Good. Jamie can drop him off later—"

"No." What about their arrangement didn't she understand? Dalton was *not* okay with Jamie dropping off his son. He'd never be okay with it. He surveyed the cold terrain. Cows mooing in the distance. A hawk perched on a fencepost up ahead. And he willed himself to stay calm. "We've been through this. Our custody arrangement is legally binding."

"Well, I can't drop him off. I have a hair appointment."

"I'm already doing *you* the favor." His voice rose. Who did she think she was?

"Don't yell at me," she whispered.

He wanted to hurl the phone to the next county when she did that. She was good at acting like a wounded animal. And he was equally good at taking her bait. They'd played their roles for years, and he was tired of it. Tired of being the bad guy.

"I tell you what," he said. "I'll pick him up tonight after supper."

She didn't answer, and his hands grew colder as Sugarpie lifted one front hoof, then the other, ready to continue back.

"Fine, if you get him tonight," she said, "we'll pick him up Sunday afternoon."

"You mean *you'll* pick him up Sunday afternoon."

"Do you ever get tired of being so childish?" she snapped.

"I'll see you tonight." And he hung up. Then he clicked his tongue and nudged Sugarpie to head back. The cold no longer bit at him—he was too hot and upset to notice it.

Childish? She thought he was the one being childish? For not wanting to see her gushing all over her new husband every time they exchanged Grady? What was childish about agreeing to take the boy for a long weekend on very short notice *and* being the one to pick him up when she lived almost an hour away?

If anyone was being childish, it was her. A hair appointment. He shook his head in disgust. She could have canceled her dumb appointment. And to hear the lilt in her voice about how Jamie had surprised her with a trip? It chafed him. Positively chafed him.

Dalton had never been able to afford to surprise her with a vacation, even a short one. His ranch had never been very profitable. He'd scraped by every year. And she'd been accustomed to an upper-middle-class lifestyle. Asking her to forgo buying expensive new clothes or reduce the number of trips to the salon had shamed him. When he did tell her they couldn't afford it? She never argued. She'd merely hang her head as if embarrassed to be living that way. Then, she'd go behind his back and do it, anyhow…on her own personal credit card. When he found out about it, it had bothered him that he couldn't give her the lifestyle she deserved. It was part of the reason he hadn't put up a fight when she took the sales job with Jamie's company shortly after Grady was born.

Stop dwelling on the past.

It was over. Their marriage, their life together, was over. He didn't need to think about it now.

Twenty minutes later, he'd taken care of Sugarpie and settled himself in the office chair. He took the checklist out of the drawer and reviewed it before Erica arrived. He still needed to leave detailed instructions for Lars and Sam for the weekend.

"Oh, good, you're here. I have so many ideas for the bake sale." Erica swept inside, her eyes aglow and dimples popping as she shut the door and took a seat. She slapped a notebook on his desk before taking off her gloves and hat. "Crank up the space heater, will you?"

Seeing those dimples as she pointed to the space heater behind him put him in a better mood. He swiveled and bumped up the temperature.

"So here's what I'm thinking." She clicked a pen, leaned forward and pointed to boxes on the paper. "We'll have the bake sale tables lined up in the center. And on the outskirts, we'll set up the tables for the bazaar."

"What about this side of the pole barn?" He pointed to the left, which was a huge empty space.

She bit the corner of her bottom lip. "I don't know. Leave it empty?"

"Seems a waste, don't you think?" He thought about things he'd looked forward to as a young kid. His grandparents had taken him and his brother to see Santa, and there had been hot cocoa and popcorn. There'd even been a small area to pet bunnies. He'd loved going every year. "Who usually attends the bake sale?"

"Everyone. Last year, most of the town showed up. It's something fun to do to get into the Christmas spirit."

"Kids, too?"

"Oh, yes."

"Could you do something to make it special for them? Hire a Santa? Have some refreshments? Maybe bring in some animals for the kids to pet. My brother and I used to go to a local farm that had a Santa, and we'd pet bunnies there."

"Yes, we *need* bunnies." Her eyes practically popped out of her head they grew so wide. "What a great idea! Someone around here must have baby goats or lambs or other cute animals for the kids to pet. Oh, and let's get reindeer! I love this!"

She grabbed the notebook and began writing furiously.

"And in the spirit of Christmas," she said, looking up momentarily, "I think we should put out a freewill donation jar to help raise money for the community center repairs."

"That's a good idea."

"I'll talk to Christy about it. This is so great."

Dalton couldn't drag his gaze away from her animated face.

"We're going to need more tables and chairs. Christmas trees. Hay. Space for the reindeer. Decorations. A lot of decorations."

Once more, she began writing.

"Where are you going to find reindeer?"

She glanced up, a slow grin spreading across her face. "I don't know, but I'll find them."

Erica would undoubtedly find them. The woman was determined. Her enthusiasm was contagious.

They went back and forth with ideas for several minutes, and then they discussed the ranch's checklist.

"I was planning on staying here and working all weekend, but there's been a change in plans." Dalton leaned back, blowing out a breath. "I'm going to have Grady."

"You are?"

"Yeah, I guess Jamie surprised Haley with a trip to Utah."

She stiffened, all her previous animation dissolving. "I see."

"I'm picking up Grady tonight."

"I know you planned on staying here, but again, you're welcome to join me in Sunrise Bend. The meal will be a jeans-splitter—I can promise you that. Grady and Rowan will love playing with my nieces. And it's just for the day. I'll be coming back tomorrow night."

It was on the tip of his tongue to decline. But why? There was zero chance of running into Jamie there. And Grady did get along great with Rowan. Why shouldn't they enjoy a big meal at Erica's family's house?

The extra people would provide a buffer, and the boys would have fun. He wouldn't be alone on the holiday, the way he'd been the past two years. Besides, he had no food here to make a feast for his son, and he didn't have the skills to cook one if he did.

"You talked me into it."

"Really?" Her happy face made him smile. "This is perfect. We can talk more about the bake sale on the drive there."

"Don't you think it's more than a bake sale at this point?"

"You're right. It's a full-on Christmas extravaganza."

He laughed. "That it is."

Their eyes met, and something warm and sweet grew between them.

He liked Erica. More than he should.

He was the first to break eye contact. "I guess I'll see you tomorrow, then."

"Bright and early."

He was growing too close to her. But he couldn't pretend they'd ever have a future together beyond boss and employee.

Oh, why was he worrying? One Thanksgiving together wasn't going to change anything. And planning a Christmas extravaganza together wouldn't, either. He'd be careful with his heart. He couldn't let himself get hurt again.

Chapter Seven

"So what's going on with you and Dalton?"

Erica set down her mug and rolled her eyes at her sister-in-law Sienna, who'd asked the question. They were sitting at the large table in her parents' dining room with her mom, Reagan and Holly late in the afternoon. They'd finished eating Thanksgiving dinner an hour ago. Jet and Blaine were taking Dalton out for a *quick tour* of the ranch. She knew how her brothers worked. There would be nothing quick about it.

Her dad was currently on the couch in the family room with one arm around Rowan and the other around Grady. Clara and Elizabeth, Holly and Jet's five-year-old and three-year-old daughters, along with Madeline, Sienna and Blaine's three-year-old daughter, had snuggled together on the love seat with a fluffy pink throw over their legs. They were watching *A Charlie Brown Christmas.* Every child in the room had drooping eyelids. Erica gave it five minutes, tops, before every one of them was asleep. Including her dad.

"I'm surprised you waited this long to ask." Erica gestured to her mom to pass the tub of whipped cream. Mom slid it her way, and she dolloped another scoop on her half-eaten slice of pumpkin pie. "He's my new ranch manager and an overall nice guy. The end. Let's get back to Reagan. What was that flavor combination you haven't mastered?"

"Dark chocolate and cayenne truffles." Reagan popped a bite of pie in her mouth, chewed and held up her fork. "But I think there's more to this Dalton thing than you're letting on."

Erica should have known they'd read more into her bringing him here. In fact, she had known it, but she'd figured they all understood she couldn't possibly get involved with him. For multiple reasons.

"Come on, guys," Erica said. "You know there's nothing there. We have a solid working relationship. The ranch is being well taken care of. Obviously, that's all there is to it."

"Good." Mom brushed crumbs from the table into her cupped hand. "He's very nice—"

"And handsome," Holly added.

"A hottie, for sure," Sienna chimed in.

"He is gorgeous, Erica," Reagan said, shrugging innocently.

"But—" Mom had her stern face on as she looked from woman to woman until she reached Erica "—there's baggage."

"Exactly." Erica gave her mother a firm nod. Who would have thought they'd be in agreement on this? But she had a feeling they weren't. It was the way her tummy went topsy-turvy. And the little voice of dissent was whispering in her ear the way it always did when she and her mother weren't on the same page. It asked why shouldn't she be able to explore a relationship with Dalton? They were both adults. Both single.

"Yes, well, the baggage is not insurmountable." Holly pursed her lips.

"If he makes you happy, you should go for it." Reagan's pretty face glowed. Erica wanted to give her a hug.

"Sometimes, you just know." With a soft smile, Sienna rubbed her six-month baby bump.

"And sometimes it's best to take things slow," Mom said. Worry lines etched her forehead. "To wait. Give yourself time to really know what you're getting into. Just because you have your exes in common, doesn't mean you have other things in common, too."

Erica drew her eyebrows together. What was Mom getting at? "Um, okay? This isn't about our exes. And I never said we have anything in common. We're not taking things slow or fast or in between because we're not a thing. Do you guys even listen to a word I say?"

Holly exchanged a charged glance with Sienna. Her mother looked skeptical.

Reagan, sitting next to her, patted her forearm. "Sorry, Erica."

"No need to be sorry." She gave her sister her warmest smile. "I miss you. Will you at least consider opening a chocolate shop in Jewel River? You have the building and everything."

While Erica had inherited Winston Ranch from Great-Aunt Martha, Reagan had inherited Dewey's company, MDW Management, and was the proud owner of three commercial buildings and a small house in downtown Jewel River, along with the company's cash assets.

"I don't know." Reagan averted her gaze, lifting her shoulders in a slight shrug. "I still have a few months of training to complete."

"I hope you'll move back here." Mom smiled at Reagan.

Were those tears in her eyes? Erica peered more closely. Yep. Their mother missed Reagan, which wasn't surprising since those two had worked side by side for years making candles. A jab of jealousy sliced through her. Mom didn't seem overly upset about Erica not being around.

There was no doubt the woman loved Erica. But her mother and Reagan had always shared a creative side that Erica lacked.

"Well, I don't care what anyone says, I think Dalton's perfect for you." Sienna waggled her eyebrows at Erica. "He kept sneaking peeks your way during dinner."

"I noticed that, too." Holly eagerly nodded. "And Jet and Blaine *lo-o-ove* him. I mean it took them all of what, five minutes, to drag him out to the stables? I wouldn't be surprised if they were giving him the full tour of both ranches as we speak."

Erica perked up at their cheerful attitudes. This was why she adored them both.

Mom made a tsking sound.

Here we go.

"What?" Erica was getting tired of her mother's attitude. "What's wrong now? What bad decision are you trying to prevent me from making?"

Her eyes flashed wide. "I'm not—"

"Yes, you are." Erica shouldn't be getting into it with her. Not here. Not now. But it got old, feeling like she was being judged and found lacking.

"Are either of you ready for a relationship? You both went through a lot with the divorces. And any romance with Dalton would naturally include Haley." Her mother clenched the napkin in her hand and frowned. "I don't know if being around her is what's best for you."

Yes, because Haley was perfect and Erica was not.

As if she needed the reminder. "Got it, Mom. Haley's a gourmet meal, and I'm leftover sloppy joes."

"That's not what I meant."

"Sure it isn't." She was *this* close to joining the guys outside.

"I'm merely saying that if you and Dalton ended up together, you'd be forced to be around his ex more than you already are. The situation is difficult enough. A clean break would be best for you. If you want to start dating, there are plenty of good men out there."

Erica brought her hands to her face and started rubbing her cheeks. "I don't want to start dating. I invited Dalton here because he's alone. He has no family. And he ended up having Grady last-minute. I figured he'd enjoy a big Thanksgiving meal. You and Dad know how to whip up a feast. I wish you'd stop reading more into it."

This was why she lived in Jewel River.

This was why she wasn't moving back to Sunrise Bend. Ever.

Her mom would always see her as an incompetent little girl, incapable of making good decisions.

"I need some air." She pushed the half-eaten pie away from her and almost tipped over the chair as she stood.

A few minutes later, she'd hauled on her winter coat and was marching outside. It had started snowing earlier, and the flakes drifted haphazardly in the air.

The creak of the door opening made her stiffen. She didn't bother turning around to see who it was.

"Honey—" Her mother, draped in a plaid shawl, picked her way down the porch steps.

"Don't, Mom." Erica clenched her jaw and wrapped her coat more tightly around her body.

"I'm sorry." She joined her and faced the pasture where

Erica was staring at nothing but dead grass and cows in the distance. "I shouldn't have jumped to conclusions. You did the right thing—inviting him here. I don't know why I get like this."

The jagged edges of her hurt feelings began to soften. "You get like this because you think I have bad judgment."

"That's not true."

Erica turned to face her. "It is true. You didn't like Jamie. You didn't think I should marry him. You didn't like me quitting the candle company to work for him. You didn't think I should move to Casper, and you certainly didn't want me to live on Winston Ranch."

"It wasn't that I didn't like Jamie." Mom shivered. "I wanted him to be a better man. He always put himself first, and you deserved better than that."

"I'm not disagreeing with you." Why was this conversation suddenly so hard to have?

"Dad and I understood when you moved to Casper and quit the company. You were married. It was the right thing to do. We weren't convinced managing the dealership would be fulfilling for you, but we didn't fault you for doing it."

Her throat felt like a vise was squeezing it.

"I still wish you'd come back here. Not because I think you can't handle Winston Ranch—you're more than capable—but because I'm selfish. I like having you around. You have a lot of energy. You say exactly what's on your mind. And you're sassy—I miss having that sass here. It's fun."

Wait, her mom was actually paying her a compliment?

"You'd get tired of sassy real quick." Erica attempted to smile but was pretty sure she failed.

"No. Never." Mom put her arm around Erica's waist and gave her a side-hug. "I miss you. I love you. I want you to have so much more than what you currently have."

"What do you mean? I have the most adorable son in the world, a thriving ranch and I get to be completely selfish now that Jamie's out of the picture."

Her mother let go, and she instantly missed her soft warmth.

"What I said in there—" Mom gathered the shawl around her shoulders "—had nothing to do with Dalton. He's a very nice man. A strong cowboy. He's a good father. It's obvious."

"I agree."

"My concern has everything to do with both of your divorces. That's it."

"I know, Mom. Trust me, I'm well aware of it being impossible." She thought she believed it to be true until it came out of her mouth. Why was the thought of a relationship with Dalton impossible?

Sure, it would be awkward, but...

"Just be careful." Her mother took a deep breath and turned toward the house. "I'm going back in before I catch a cold."

"I'm going to stay out here another minute."

As her mother went back inside, Erica didn't even try to decipher the waves of emotions lapping at her heart. She'd needed to hear her mother's apology...and her point of view. It did make her feel better knowing that her mom missed her. Plus, her worries about Dalton were justified, even though Erica wished they weren't.

It was starting to hit her that she really *was* attracted to Dalton more than she'd realized. They were growing closer every day. Or maybe they were both just lonely.

It didn't matter. She needed to be more careful. As usual, her mother was right.

The sun was setting as Dalton drove away from Sunrise Bend. Erica sat in the passenger seat of his truck, and the boys were strapped in their car seats behind them. She looked pensive. Scratch that. She'd *been* pensive ever since he and her brothers came back inside after they'd shown him around the ranch. Was she mad that he'd gone off with them?

Haley had always given him the silent treatment when he'd done something she didn't like. And she wouldn't have liked him leaving her inside while he headed out with the guys.

He clutched the steering wheel and flipped on the radio. An instrumental Christmas song was playing. It wasn't like he owed Erica anything if she *was* mad at him. They weren't a couple. They were friends. And it had been really nice being her friend today.

Her brothers were his kind of guys. The three of them had talked horses, cows, pastures and football all afternoon. Jet and Blaine were family men and as into ranching as he was. Plus, Erica's parents had been so warm and welcoming, he'd felt like he'd stepped into a movie, one where everything was perfect. At least for a day.

The Thanksgiving meal itself had been the best he'd ever eaten. A succulent turkey, homemade stuffing, every vegetable and side dish imaginable. And the pies? Pumpkin, apple, pecan. He could have eaten for days. His belt felt tighter just thinking about it.

"Thanks for inviting me." Dalton glanced at Erica, bracing himself for her to ignore him.

Instead, she gave him a bright smile. "I'm glad you came. I hope my brothers weren't too overbearing."

She was glad he came? The gleam in her eyes made him believe her.

"They weren't overbearing at all. I liked them."

"Good." She twisted to check the back seat. "Keeping up with all those girls must have worn our boys out. They're both asleep already."

"Yeah, your parents will sleep good tonight, too." Dalton was still amused thinking about the games her parents had played with the kids. Musical chairs, beanbag toss, red-light green-light. The kids had run around their family room shouting and laughing for the past hour and a half. "They sure did entertain them all."

"They love it. Love being grandparents."

Dalton could tell. His own grandparents had been strict but loving. He couldn't say he'd ever thought of them as fun, though.

Erica's pensive expression returned, and she stared out her window again. Something must be bothering her.

He should leave it alone. Shouldn't ask if anything was wrong. What if she told him what he didn't want to hear? That having him with her had spoiled her holiday? But the words tumbled to his tongue, anyway. "Is anything wrong?"

"What?" She startled, glancing his way. "Oh, no. I was just thinking."

"About what?" He couldn't shake the feeling he was to blame for…whatever was bothering her.

"About my life. The choices I've made."

"Oh."

"Mom and I had an argument."

He wasn't sure he wanted to know what it was about.

"It was about you," she said.

Just as he'd feared.

"And it reminded me I haven't always made the best decisions. But, well… I don't know. I don't think I'd do anything differently if given the chance. Does that make sense?"

Not really.

"What choices are we talking about?" And how did they relate to him being the subject of the argument with her mother?

"Marrying Jamie. Managing his dealership. Ignoring the signs he was cheating on me."

Oh, now he got it.

"For what it's worth, I had no idea Haley was cheating on me. None."

"Wish I could say the same." She sighed. "I had these tingly warnings. Like, I knew something wasn't right. But I didn't want to believe it. I chalked it up to my pregnancy or overreacting to all the time he was spending on the road."

For the first time, Dalton considered how Jamie and Haley's infidelity had affected Erica. He'd placed her in the box of "Divorce: Don't Touch" without thinking about her feelings.

"I never told anyone this, but I tried to get Jamie to stay with me. I knew he was in love with Haley, and I still begged him to stay. I thought it wasn't fair for Rowan to not have both parents together, and I wasn't ready to give up on my picture of what life should be. To be honest, I was still in love with him at the time. How pathetic."

Dalton let everything sink in and loosened his grip on the steering wheel. He'd never seen Erica this vulnerable.

"I don't talk about it," she said, flicking her fingernail

with her thumb. "I don't know why I'm telling you now. You must think I'm a fool."

"The last thing I'd ever think is that you're a fool." The barbed wire he'd wound around his heart loosened a bit. "I tried to get Haley to stay, too. For all the same reasons. Plus, one other one." He didn't want to admit what it was. It embarrassed him.

"You didn't want Jamie to win." She glanced his way, lifting one shoulder in the process. "I didn't want Haley to win, either."

How did she know? How could she possibly know exactly how he'd felt?

"I still fight it—that awful, mean rock in my heart that doesn't want them to be happy…" Her voice tapered off at the end. "I pray about it, but I don't pray with much enthusiasm, you know? I mean, I was the one they wronged. Why should I feel guilty?"

"I feel it, too." He nodded more to himself than to her. "I push them out of my mind, and then Haley will text me with another request for money for something for Grady. I get so mad. She's over there going on with her life like she didn't do anything wrong, and I'm stuck paying for things I never agreed to."

"Well, Jamie's got enough money. Tell her he can pay for it."

He swallowed the sour taste in his mouth. "But it's my kid. I can provide for my son."

"I see your point." Her head wobbled back and forth slightly as she considered. "But you pay child support, right? She should be responsible for any extra expenses."

He thought so, too, but he didn't want to discuss it further. It made him feel like a pushover. He stared into the darkness. The headlights revealed the empty highway lined by the prairie. Christmas music still played quietly in the otherwise silent truck.

"Mom thought I brought you to the ranch because you and I are interested in each other. I told her it's not like that."

He'd all but forgotten about her argument with her mother. He'd thought he'd made a decent impression, but clearly, her mom didn't like him. Could he blame the woman, though? Erica had it all—style, charm, a thriving cattle ranch—and what did he have to offer her? Nothing.

"She's worried we'll get close." Erica leaned the side of her head into her palm. "Working together. Becoming friends. She has a point. Our baggage could hurt us both."

"By baggage, I take it you mean Haley and Jamie?"

She nodded. He wanted to reach over and comfort her, but he kept both hands on the wheel. Touching her would be a mistake.

"Well, it's a good thing we're not interested in each other like that." As soon as the words were out of his mouth, he berated himself. *Liar.* He *was* interested. He couldn't deny it.

"That's what I told her."

He should be relieved, but regret was all he felt. She didn't like him the way he liked her. And why would she?

"Besides," Erica said, "we both agreed this was a weird situation, and we need to avoid our exes. If anything more were to grow between us, spending time with them would be unavoidable."

"Maybe." He should agree with her. Should nix this attraction right now. But he couldn't.

"What do you mean?" She gave him a curious look.

"I mean, my custody arrangement is legally binding. It stands regardless if I date someone or get married."

Erica considered his statement, then nodded. "Mine, too."

"I've just never dated." He suddenly wondered if Erica had.

"Me, neither."

Relief trickled through his body. Stupid, really, to react this strongly over a woman he couldn't have.

"Look, your mom is right. Our relationship is complicated enough. You're my boss. You were married to my ex-wife's husband. We both have kids. I'm glad we get along, but we both have too much to lose by even thinking beyond our current relationship." He couldn't believe he was having this conversation with her. He tended to bury his feelings. Pretend they weren't real.

After a deep inhale and a loud exhalation, she nodded. "You're right. I'm thankful we get along well. You're doing a great job at managing the ranch, and we'll have no trouble working together on the Christmas extravaganza. I can count on you."

As she snuggled back into the seat, he frowned. She seemed perfectly content with him as the manager and them being friends. And he should be content with it, too. But the extra time together getting ready for the Christmas event could tip his heart in the direction he didn't want it to go. And then what would he do?

He needed to lock down these feelings before he got hurt.

Chapter Eight

"I've got another load of tables, missy."

Erica looked up from her clipboard to see Clem standing before her in the pole barn on Saturday morning, a week after Thanksgiving. His coat was open, revealing a red flannel shirt tucked into jeans. His weathered face and gleaming eyes were all business. She and Dalton had worked late all week planning and organizing the Christmas event. She'd called the legacy club about helping with the initial setup today, and several members had stopped by to lend a hand.

"Thanks, Clem." She gave him a big smile. "Dalton, Marc, Cade and Ty should be outside. They'll unload them for you."

"That Zane woman is driving me bonkers." He hadn't moved a muscle. "She calls two, three times a week with harebrained ideas. Do you know what the latest one is?"

"No." Erica prepared herself for the unimaginable.

"Shakespearean theater. In the park." He didn't so much as blink.

"Oh, my." She scrunched her nose. That was a bit much. "What did you tell her?"

"This is Wyoming, not England, and no one here is going to dress up in tights. We don't have a place to do it, anyhow."

"Did she back off?" She lowered her arm to her side, the clipboard still in hand.

"No. She then got the bright idea that we needed an auditorium. To move the Shakespeare doohickey indoors." He ran his tongue over his teeth. "I can't have her on my committee anymore. You take her."

No way. Erica sympathized with Clem—really, she did—but she was not taking Angela off his hands.

"As I mentioned before, Mary keeps me busy enough."

"She can't be as bad as Angela."

"Oh, you'd be surprised." Erica scanned the area to make sure no one was eavesdropping. Most of the helpers had left since they were almost finished with the setup. "Here are the calls I've gotten. Dog park. Poetry club. Permanent equipment to make kettle corn in the park— I mean, really? Who would operate it? It can't be safe. Let's see, what else? Zip lines linking the abandoned buildings at the old tool-and-die company. As you can see, my hands, too, are full."

"I see your point." He ran two fingers along the rim of his hat. "Maybe they could be their own committee. Just the two of them."

"I thought of that, but last year Mary accused Angela of stealing her angel-food-cake recipe, and Angela told her she'd never steal a recipe for a cake that didn't even taste good, and, well, you can see the problem."

"Fine." Clem glowered at her. "I'll go find that man of yours."

Man of hers? "He's my manager, not my man."

"Whatever you say, missy." Clem was already walking away.

She turned her attention back to the clipboard. They'd borrowed every table from town they could, and she'd purchased more to be delivered on Wednesday. The Christmas trees were in stands, thanks to Sam and Johnny Abbot, who'd gravitated to each other on account of being distant relatives.

Eight trees in all. And they all needed decorations. And lights. Lots of lights.

She jotted another note on her list. She'd been running nonstop since eight o'clock this morning. It was a good thing she'd dropped off Rowan at Jamie's last night. He'd tried to goad her into an argument about hiring Dalton, and she'd completely ignored him. He had no say in her life anymore, and she wasn't going to pretend he did. The fact that he'd gotten mad when she turned to leave and tossed out "You think this is getting back at me somehow, but the joke's on you. Haley told me he was never good at ranching" had only made her shake her head.

Whom was she going to believe? Every rancher in the county? Or her lying, cheating ex-husband? The choice was clear.

"Erica?"

She whirled to see who had called her name. Christy Moulten was pulling on her gloves, and Cade was behind her.

"We're going to take off." Christy came up and gave her a quick hug. "This is so impressive. I never realized how big this barn was. Martha sure knew how to go big or go home, am I right?"

"She sure did." Erica grinned. "Thank you so much for all your help. And thank you, too, Cade."

"No problem." He gave her a nod and addressed his mom. "Are you ready?"

"Where's Ty?"

"He left a few minutes ago."

"Always in a hurry." Christy wrapped a scarf around her neck. "Now, before we leave, Erica, what are you going to do about decorating all those trees?"

"On my list." She tapped her pen against the clipboard. "We still need someone to volunteer to run the hot cocoa stand."

"I'll talk to Janie Fry. She heads up the honor society at the high school. Those kids are always looking for volunteer opportunities."

"Oh, good." Erica brightened. "If she has enough volunteers, ask her if any would run the popcorn machine."

"The youth group at church might help out." Her eyebrows drew together. "Have you heard back from the Smiths about the petting zoo?"

"No."

"You should have Angela Zane call them," Cade said.

Erica and Christy turned to him. "Why?"

He shrugged. "I don't know. It's hard to get off the phone with Angela, and they'll probably agree to anything just to end the call."

Erica stared at Christy, and they both let out a hearty laugh.

"Brilliant," Erica said. "I'll have Clem ask Angela to call them."

"Clem?" Christy's eyebrows soared to her hairline. "You're a brave woman asking him for a favor."

They said their goodbyes and walked away. Erica massaged her shoulders and stretched her neck from side to side. She should run outside before Clem left.

That's when she remembered. The reindeer.

Ugh. She'd forgotten to call the farmer in Casper who raised them. Christy had given her the contact information a few days ago. Erica checked the time. Almost five. Too late now.

She crossed the space to the door and halted at the blast of wind in her face. Hugging her arms, she ran to where she spotted Clem getting into his truck.

"Clem, wait," she yelled, running faster. She finally reached the truck, and he rolled down the window. "Would you do me a favor? Would you please call Angela and ask her to call the Smiths? We're trying to line up a petting zoo for the kids."

Her teeth chattered as she waited for his response, which she assumed would be "call her yourself."

"That's a good idea. It'll get her off my back." Clem smiled—he actually smiled!—and lifted his hand in goodbye, then rolled up the window. She stepped aside so he could drive away. His was the last vehicle to leave.

She turned and Dalton was standing behind her.

"Come on, let's get inside before we freeze to death." He hitched his thumb to the pole barn. They both jogged to the door. Once inside, it took her a few minutes to stop shivering.

"We got a lot done today," he said, pulling out a folding chair near the table full of red pillar candles one of the ladies had dropped off. "You sure have good friends."

"I do. But I can't take credit. They're all members of the Jewel River Legacy Club." She took out a chair, too, and practically sank into it.

"What's that?"

She filled him in on the basics. "We're in the initial phases of figuring out the town's needs. When we have a better idea of what to do, we'll make a plan to start addressing them."

"You're the one who came up with the club?" He leaned back in his chair and stacked his ankle on the other knee. His hands were folded on his lap.

"I guess. It sort of fell into place when I started calling around to figure out what to do with this place." She waved her arm to represent the pole barn. "Did I tell you about my aunt's letter?"

"No."

"She left me a letter telling me she wanted me to do something with the pole barn—to start a business from my heart, one that would help the people of Jewel River."

His thoughtful expression gave her hope that she really would figure out what to do with it.

"I knew you were trying to figure out what to do with the pole barn, but I didn't know your aunt's wishes. What have you come up with?"

"Um...nothing?" It wasn't for lack of brainstorming. "I haven't stumbled onto the right business yet. I'm hoping an idea will strike me soon."

"How soon?" His lazy smile sent flutters through her stomach.

"Within the next couple of months."

"Whatever you decide, you'll be great at it."

"You think so?" She, personally, had doubts. Her work experience consisted of managing two family businesses. She'd fallen into each job. Did she have the skills to run her own business? One from scratch?

"Of course," he said. "Look at how you've headed up the Christmas extravaganza."

Her mood lightened at his use of the word *extrava-*

ganza. They'd been teasing each other about their pet name for the event all week.

"Well," she said, "the expansion was your idea—a very good one, at that."

"You're allowed to take credit for this, you know," he said. "And for creating the legacy club. And for making good decisions regarding the ranch."

Her chest felt tight. She couldn't take credit for any of it. It was what anyone would do.

"No." She averted her gaze and shook her head. "I was at the right place at the right time."

"You get things done." Dalton set his foot back on the ground and leaned forward. "You say yes when most people would say no."

But was she saying yes to the right things? Maybe she should be saying no more often. Her life was a merry-go-round of to-dos at this point.

"I appreciate it, Dalton, I do. But I feel like I've been falling into things most of my life. Shouldn't I have a purpose? Like everyone else does?"

"I'm not sure what you mean."

"When my mom and Reagan started making candles, I joined them because I worried they wouldn't set up the business correctly. They're both supercreative, but neither of them wanted to deal with basic things like filing the necessary paperwork with the state or figuring out an invoicing system."

"I'm not good at any of that stuff, either." He winced.

"Nor was I, but I figured out what needed to be done."

"Exactly. You did it."

"And then Jamie wanted me to manage his Casper dealership when we got married."

"What's wrong with that?"

"I never stopped and asked myself if I wanted to manage it. I just wanted him to be happy. And now I inherited this amazing ranch along with this pole barn. I have the freedom to do anything I want with it. And what am I doing?"

He waited for her answer, but she didn't have one. She threw her hands in the air and let her back rest against the chair.

"Nothing. I'm clueless."

"You'll figure it out."

Would she, though? She didn't know.

"Are you praying about it?" he asked.

"Umm... I wouldn't say I'm actively praying about it. Did I pray a few times after Great-Aunt Martha died? Sure. But..." Guilt nipped at her conscience. She went to church every week. Read a few verses of the Bible most days. But she hadn't been praying much lately.

"It's never too late to pray about it." Dalton stood, groaning as he stretched out his back. "I don't know about you, but I'm hungry."

"Same here." She stood, too, and took in the pole barn. Tables were set up willy-nilly around the room. The Christmas trees were grouped together in their stands. Boxes of various items—paper goods, Styrofoam cups, rolls of plastic to cover the tables—were stacked against the wall next to the kitchen door. "Did you have plans for supper?"

He shook his head. They found their coats and made their way to the door. "I have a wild night ahead of me. I'm decorating my Christmas tree and eating a grilled cheese with tomato soup. You're welcome to join me."

"That's okay. I have a wild night of my own planned." He held the door open for her and closed it after they'd both exited. They fell in step with each other, heads down due to the wind, as they crossed the gravel parking lot to the path that led to the main house.

"If you change your mind, give me a call," she said when she reached her porch. She hoped he would, but it would be better if he didn't.

"Okay."

Another lonely Saturday night loomed ahead of her. Maybe the flurry of activity was to avoid the loneliness of her weekends when Rowan wasn't around.

She didn't need company to be happy. But it sure would have been nice if Dalton had said yes.

Two hours later, Dalton stepped back to make sure the small pine he'd cut yesterday in the woods was straight. It was a short, fat tree, and it made him chuckle every time he looked at it.

He padded to the back utility room, where he'd stored his lone container of Christmas decorations. Haley had taken most of them in the divorce, and he hadn't cared. Hadn't wanted any of it. He'd known it would only remind him of happier holidays, when they'd been together. This was the first time he was decorating a tree since their divorce. His heart hadn't been into it until this year.

After hauling the bin into the living room, he realized how little he actually had. Three balled-up strings of white lights; none of them looked like they worked. A ratty wreath with a plaid bow dangling by a thread. A plastic baggie with a few chipped silver bulbs. And that was it.

A surge of anger rose in his belly. She'd taken everything except three barely usable strands of lights, some chipped bulbs and a wreath that should have been trashed. It showed her contempt for him.

Shaking his head, he started unraveling the lights. The television was playing *Home Alone* for the millionth time, not that he minded. It provided background noise. Made him feel less lonely.

And right now he could admit to himself that, yes, he felt lonely.

He hadn't been able to stop thinking about Erica all week. After their conversation on the way home from her parents' house on Thanksgiving, they'd spent the rest of last weekend separately, except for a few hours on Saturday when the boys played together. Their afternoon meetings every day had proceeded as usual. Easy and drama-free.

And tonight…well, he'd been surprised what she'd revealed about not thinking she had a purpose. That she believed she'd fallen into her jobs.

Didn't she have a clue how talented she was? How rare it was for someone to see a need and offer to fill it?

Erica cared about people. Her son. Her employees. Gemma. The people of Jewel River. The crafters and bakers selling their holiday items. The kids and families who were going to show up to the Christmas event…er, extravaganza.

He found it refreshing that she spoke exactly what was on her mind. She didn't hide anything. She was willing to be vulnerable.

And all the things she'd mentioned about her marriage? He'd put them in his heart. Because he understood her pain. He just wasn't equipped to share it the way she did.

Dalton didn't like to think back to the period of time

when Haley had grown close to Jamie. It had been shortly after Grady's birth. Four months, maybe. He remembered how out of character it had been when she told him she needed a break from the baby. That Jamie Black had offered her a sales rep position, and she'd already lined up a babysitter.

Dalton had been blindsided.

Haley had never worked during their marriage. The timing was strange. A few months after their baby was born? She suddenly wanted a job? One that required her to travel the occasional weekend?

He'd laid out his concerns, mostly about her being away from Grady. But she'd assured him she'd only be gone a weekend here or there, and the job was part time. When he'd hesitated to give her an answer, she'd done that thing where she folded her hands in her lap and her eyes went downcast. Her entire posture had been one of defeat. And he'd felt like an absolute jerk. So he'd gone along with it.

And a month later, he'd realized the traveling was a lot more extensive than she'd let on. Whenever she'd come home after one of the business trips, she'd have a glow about her...until she settled back into their small one-story ranch house. It was as if a gray cloud descended on her within an hour.

He'd chalked it up to her excitement about being employed. Not that she ever contributed to their household expenses. Nope. She'd bought herself expensive clothes. Toys for Grady. Lots of things. It had gone on for a year before she asked for the divorce.

Her betrayal still hurt him. The fact that he'd refused to see the signs still bothered him, too.

He tossed aside the ball of lights in frustration. He

needed to stop thinking about it. Needed to get over it already. Needed to get over *her*.

His words to Erica earlier floated in his mind. *Are you praying about it?*

She, at least, had the grace to admit she wasn't actively praying about it.

Much like he'd pushed away any suspicions about Haley when they were married, he pushed away praying about the situation, too. He didn't know what to pray for.

They'd been divorced for almost two years. Haley was remarried. They weren't getting back together.

Dalton reached for one of the tangled balls of lights again, and this time, he slowly, methodically unraveled it. *God, I need help. I'm still upset about the divorce. I'm mad at myself for putting up blinders where Haley was concerned. And I think I'm mad that she's happy, while I'm stuck.*

Was that true, though? Not anymore.

He wasn't stuck. He was living on Winston Ranch. Riding Sugarpie every day. Managing a huge, successful cattle operation. Providing for his son.

Lord, I don't know what's wrong with me. I don't know why I can't seem to get over Haley. Or why I'm attracted to Erica, when she's clearly all wrong for me. I'm her employee. She used to be married to Jamie. Am I an idiot? Stumbling into another mistake?

His phone chimed, and he uncurled his legs to stand. Grabbed it from the counter. Erica's name appeared on the screen, and he read her text.

So it appears I have a Christmas decoration addiction. If you need any ornaments, you know where to find them.

His thumbs launched into motion. I have none.

None? How is that possible?

Instead of anger or regret, joy bubbled up inside him. He replied, Because I wimped out in the divorce.

He couldn't take it back. Had never admitted, even to himself, how much of a pushover he'd been. And instead of feeling shame, he felt giddy.

Or you didn't like the decorations. Laughing emoji.

He chuckled. Leave it to Erica to find the right thing to say.

Can I come over now and get some of them? He held his breath as the dots moved while she typed.

Only if you help me put the star on top of my tree.

Done.

Erica paced the front hall as she waited for Dalton to arrive. Her heartbeat was thumping harder than a scared rabbit's hind foot when in danger. She shouldn't have offered him the ornaments, even though it was true she had way too many. But after eating her grilled cheese and tomato soup, she'd opened her bins of decorations and her lungs had positively hollowed out.

Putting up the Christmas tree by herself had to rank up there as one of the saddest things she'd done in years. She should have waited for Rowan to be here with her, but with the Christmas festival in one week, she didn't have much time. From here on out, every evening would be spent in the pole barn preparing for the event. Her tree needed to be decorated tonight. She'd promised Rowan he could put the candy canes on tomorrow when he came home.

Even with her favorite Christmas playlist coming through the speaker—no "Rockin' Around the Christmas Tree" to be found—she'd fought the terrible sensation of being completely unnecessary. Like nothing she did really mattered in the grand scheme of things.

Logically, she knew it wasn't true, but she didn't have much experience with being alone. She'd be the first person to admit she was an extrovert.

Knock, knock.

Relief rushed through her, and she hustled to the door and opened it. Dalton's grin took her breath away. After letting him inside and waiting for him to take off his coat and boots, she led the way to the living room with a sense of nervous anticipation.

"I am so glad you're here." She stopped in front of the artificial tree, pre-lit with white lights. Then she turned to him. "I didn't think I'd mind decorating the tree by myself, but…"

"Yeah, I have to admit I'm not enjoying it, either."

"You're decorating your tree, too?" She wasn't sure why she was surprised. Just that he hadn't mentioned it.

"Cut one down yesterday. It's round." He puffed out his cheeks and spread his arms wide.

She laughed. "I'm guessing it smells Christmassy, unlike mine."

"It does." He bent to poke around in one of the many bins strewn across her floor. "You weren't kidding. You do have a lot of ornaments."

"What can I say? Christmas is my favorite time of the year." She spotted a crystal angel and plucked it out of the box, then held it up in front of her face. The lights glinted off it. "I bought this one with Reagan on a weekend trip to Jackson. We were supposed to be skiing, but we were rebels. We sat in the lodge and drank hot cocoa instead. And shopped, of course."

"It's pretty." He took a jolly glass Santa out of the box and held it up. "Any story with this one?"

His spicy, masculine cologne teased her senses, and she couldn't help sneaking a peek at him in his jeans and hooded sweatshirt with the University of Wyoming Cowboys logo on it. He must have changed after they'd parted ways earlier.

Everything about him appealed to her.

"A gift from my mother." Although they didn't always see eye to eye, Erica appreciated all the loving gestures from the woman. "Do you have any favorite ornaments?"

"No, I wasn't kidding when I said I don't have any." He set it back in the box and shook his head.

"None?" How could that even be possible?

"Didn't want them." Sadness softened the hard planes of his face. She had a strong urge to hug him and make him feel better. Instead, she kneeled beside the bins closest to her and began lifting out the containers of bulbs and various individual ornaments.

"I'm going to start a new collection for you." She glanced up at him with a smile. To her surprise, he got on his knees on the floor beside her.

"Not necessary. If I could borrow a few you're not using, that would be great."

Sitting back on her heels, she let the delicious thrill of giving him a starter pack fill her with a sense of purpose. Yes, now she understood why she'd bought five times the amount of ornaments she'd ever need—to share them with Dalton, who had none.

Thank You, Jesus, for making something good come out of me buying too much.

"Look, Dalton, you're doing me the favor. I've purchased way too many over the years, and trust me, I'm going to keep buying them. I won't even try to deny it. I will never be able to use them all." She pushed herself to one knee, then stood. "I'll be right back."

She needed a few plastic bags and paper towels to wrap the ornaments she was giving him. After a quick trip to the kitchen, she returned to the living room with her supplies as "Winter Wonderland" played through the speakers.

"Okay, let's see what we've got." Kneeling once more, she started going through the decorations, setting aside the ones she planned on using for her own tree and holding up the ones she'd retired. "Do you have a theme? Color preference?"

Dalton gave her a confused look. "Uh, no. I'm not picky."

Erica wasn't surprised. She leaned back slightly and placed her knuckle under her chin. "I went through a red-and-black buffalo plaid phase a few years ago. It would be perfect for you."

"Buffalos?" He smiled and shrugged. "Sounds good to me."

"Not buffalos. Buffalo plaid." She chuckled and dragged the bin over that she suspected they were in. The lid popped right off. Bingo. With both hands, she lifted out a box with a dozen shatterproof ornaments in the red-and-black plaid design. Each had a small black bow near the hook. They were supercute. "See?"

"Oh, yeah." He took the box from her. "I like them."

"Good. Oh!" She remembered the fluffy owls and

squirrels made from a strawlike material. They would add a rustic touch to his tree.

"What's wrong? Did you stab your finger on a hook or something?" He took her hand in his and inspected it. He didn't mean it to be an intimate caress, but her body didn't seem to get the memo.

"No, I just had a good idea." She almost wished she did have a cut on her finger, so he could kiss it and make it all better. He let go of her hand and waited for her to explain. "I bought the cutest owl decorations. They look like they have actual feathers. And I have tiny squirrels, too. They're made from straw or something. So cute. They would be adorable with the buffalo plaid. Trust me, Grady is going to flip over them when he stays with you."

She could picture the little boy's face. Like Rowan, he'd be delighted at seeing the cute critters on the tree.

"Like I said, you don't have to go through all this trouble…"

"Grab those boxes, will you?" Erica pointed to the stack of boxes to Dalton's left. "I'm pretty sure we'll find them in there."

He got up and hauled them over, and for the next hour, they wrapped and bagged an entire cardboard box worth of ornaments for him to take home. Additionally, she'd set aside the blue, green and purple ornaments she intended to use, as well as all the reindeer and snowmen decorations she could find. Rowan would love them.

"What's in there?" Dalton pointed to the cardboard box marked Keep.

She followed his finger. "The ones that always go on the tree no matter what. I have a small collection of Nativity ornaments. They remind me why we're celebrating. The birth of Jesus. Our sins forgiven. The promise of eternal life."

Gratitude for God's great gifts filled her.

And she remembered one other ornament she wanted Dalton to have. She dug through the Keep box until she found it. A carved wooden Nativity scene. Still on her knees and holding it in her cupped hands, she passed it to him. "I want you to have this."

"I couldn't." He shook his head. "It's meaningful to you."

"Yes, it is, because you're the one meant to have it."

"It's too much."

"It's not." She implored him with her eyes. "Please take it."

On his knees, too, he lifted his upper body to take it from her, leaving them inches apart and an invisible connection tethering them together.

Erica couldn't help glancing at his lips, then up to his eyes, which seemed to burn with intensity. Was she imagining that he wanted to kiss her? Or had she finally gotten to a point where she actually wanted a man to kiss her again? It had been so many years since she'd been attracted to anyone but Jamie.

She couldn't deny her attraction to Dalton.

But now was not the right time, not the right place... or the right man. She dropped the ornament into his hand and sat back, her heart pounding.

"Thank you." He inspected it with an awe-filled smile. It made her happy to see him happy, but it also tugged at her heart in a way she didn't like.

She wasn't ready for more. Not with him. Not with anyone.

Scrambling to her feet, she set the ornaments she didn't plan on using back into their bins. Dalton helped her. They stacked the boxes along the wall.

"Since you've been so generous with your ornaments," he said, "it's only fair I help you decorate your tree."

"You don't have to." She crossed her arms, rubbing them. "I can manage. Go ahead and take yours home."

He shook his head. "I don't think so. Let's get this tree decorated."

She might not be ready for romance, but she liked the thought of decorating together as friends.

"Okay. I'll make hot cocoa. I bought special marshmallows and everything. If we're doing this, we're doing it right."

He laughed. "Sounds good to me."

Over the next hour, they hung all the ornaments, bumping into each other, teasing each other and sharing childhood memories of Christmas the entire time. When they'd finished, Dalton placed the star on top. Then they dimmed the overhead lights to admire the tree as they brought fresh cups of cocoa to the sectional.

"We did a good job." She lifted her mug to Dalton, who reached over and clinked his with hers.

"We did."

"I wish I could have Rowan for both Christmas Eve and Christmas Day." The divorce had taken more from her than her husband. It had taken away the holidays the way she'd always imagined them, too.

"Yeah, same here with Grady." He took a sip and settled deeper into the sectional. "I'm picking him up Christmas morning."

"We have a similar arrangement." The warmth of the mug added to the cozy feel of the room. "Jamie's picking up Rowan on Saturday, and I agreed to pick him up Christmas morning."

"Are you going to your parents' on Christmas Eve?" he asked.

"No. We're celebrating on Christmas Day. I'm heading up to Sunrise Bend that afternoon. We'll spend the night there, too. What about you? What are your plans?"

"Nothing major. Church on Christmas Eve. Presents and hanging out with Grady on Christmas Day. That's about it."

"I guess we'll both be celebrating Christmas as best we can this year."

It comforted her knowing she wasn't the only one facing a less-than-perfect holiday season. She couldn't help wishing they could be there for each other. But she knew better than to open that can of worms. It was better they stuck to their plans and spent Christmas apart.

Chapter Nine

"I can't believe you pulled this off." The morning of the Christmas festival, Dalton stood next to Erica near the portable enclosure housing three reindeer. Each of the animals had festive red harnesses, and they were calmly strolling around the pen. The rising sun sent streaks of pink across the sky. The weather looked promising for the event. He was glad. For Erica's sake. She'd poured her heart and soul into getting this ready.

"I almost didn't." Erica, in a winter coat with a faux-fur-lined hood, grinned at him. "I am so thankful Christy got in touch with Jim Frankel, the owner of these guys. That woman is an endless fountain of resources."

Dalton and Erica had been working a few hours each night this week to get everything ready. Most of the legacy club members and event participants had helped the past two nights, too.

"So how will this work?" He bobbed his head to the reindeer.

"Jim will be in the enclosure the entire time. He has a few helpers. Kids must be accompanied by an adult to go in."

"Can they feed them?"

"Yes, for a dollar each. Jim has disposable cups of food available to purchase."

Dalton nodded, holding his hand over the top of the enclosure as one of the bucks came his way. He petted its forehead and couldn't help smiling. The kids were going to love this.

Gemma had kindly offered to watch both boys this morning until the event was underway. He planned on bringing Grady over later for the festivities.

Haley had dropped off Grady last night, and she'd seemed surprised to see all the vehicles at the pole barn. When he'd told her what was going on, she'd given him a tight smile and weakly admitted it would be fun for their son. Then she'd twisted her hands together and mentioned needing reimbursement for the Christmas suit she'd special-ordered for Grady.

While he hadn't been surprised she'd asked for money, Dalton had actually spoken up about it. He'd asked her why she hadn't bought an outfit for him at a local store. Her eyes had filled with tears. In the past, he'd have felt guilty. Not this time. Her reaction had merely annoyed him. She'd claimed the stores didn't have pants long enough that would fit him around the waist. He'd mentioned buying a size up, and her expression had grown hard.

He should have refused to pay for them. Why should he be responsible for her spending? But he hadn't refused. Instead, he'd offered to pay half, and she'd accepted with a curt nod. At least there'd been no sign of Jamie. After their previous encounter, Dalton hoped to never see the guy again.

"The reindeer are cute close up." A soft smile lit Erica's eyes, and her cheeks were rosy from the cold. Dalton forced his thoughts back to the present.

"Do you think Grady could feed one? Or is there an age limit?"

"Jim said as long as the parents are with the kids, it's fine. I'm bringing Rowan in." She turned away from the reindeer enclosure. "Let's check out the petting zoo and go through the pole barn one more time. Make sure we didn't forget anything."

They strode along the edge of the gravel parking lot, then popped into a large white tent, where hay bales had been arranged to make seating areas for the kids to pet bunnies, lambs and baby goats. The animals were currently being kept in the back of the tent.

"They're going to love petting these guys, too." Dalton watched the lambs curl up against each other as they napped.

"I know. I almost feel bad for all the parents who're going to be begged for a pet bunny for Christmas."

He laughed. "Grady and Rowan included."

"Yikes." She pulled a face, then chuckled. "You're right."

They continued on to the pole barn. Dalton held open the door for her and, inside, they unzipped their coats and set them on the coat tables near the entrance.

The heated barn had been transformed into a winter wonderland. All the people selling crafts and baked goods had been allowed to bring in their items last night. In the center of the room, towers of pies, breads, cookies, doughnuts and cakes were displayed on tables. The scents of pumpkin and apple and cinnamon and sugar filled the room. A row of tables had crafts for sale to the right, and another row of tables with crafts for sale was to the left. Beyond it, a large area had been set up with games and activities for the children.

"I wouldn't be surprised if Jewel River asked you to host the festival—excuse me, the extravaganza—every year after this." He approached a long table filled with blank wooden ornaments, markers, squeeze tubes of glitter glue and stickers galore. He lifted one of the ornaments, gave it a once-over and set it back down. "This is impressive."

"An annual extravaganza here. Wouldn't that be wonderful?" Erica clasped her hands to her chest. Her big brown eyes sparkled with joy. Flinging her arms out, she spun in a circle. "I love this."

His breath caught in his throat at her unabashed enthusiasm. When they first met, he never would have guessed that she was so generous. But she was. Erica seemed to thrive on making other people happy. Including him.

It humbled him. Her optimism was rare in this world.

She tugged on his sleeve. "Oh, look! One of the volunteers must have strung those twinkle lights. The wires with the small clothespins are perfect to hang up the little snapshots of the kids with Santa."

The instant camera was sitting on a table off to the side. Red tape had been applied to the floor leading to the ornate chair where Santa would be sitting. Two beautifully decorated Christmas trees flanked it, and a red velvet backdrop was draped behind the chair.

"Who's going to be Santa?" he asked.

"Johnny Abbot. I may have begged him. I'll admit it." Erica picked up the camera and inspected it. "Let's be the first picture up there." She moved her hand sideways for him to shift in front of the tree.

"No. Nope. No, thanks." He took a large step sideways toward the wall.

"Come on," she said, shaking her head. "One picture. It won't kill you."

"It might."

She chuckled and took him by the hand. Why her simple touch sent the hair on his arms rising, he wasn't going to think about. He allowed her to drag him in front of the tree. Smooshing in next to him, she held the camera an arm's length away and snapped the picture. Then she handed him the picture, set the camera on the chair and whipped out her cell phone.

"Hold that pose. I need one for my phone. Say cheese." She held her phone in the air. He refused to say cheese, but he was tempted to wrap his arm around her waist and pull her close to him. She pretended to glare at him. "Come on, Dalton. You can do it. Curve those lips into a smile. Pretend you're posing for a cowboy calendar."

He couldn't help but laugh, and her phone camera clicked in a burst of pictures.

"Are you done?" he asked, missing her closeness immediately. She slid her phone back into her pocket, plucked the photo out of his hand and began shaking it. Slowly, their faces came into view. Off-center. "I hope you have a professional taking these for the kids. Half your chin is missing."

"Yeah, well, who needs to see my cheek or chin? It's still a goodie." Smiling, she bounced over to the wall and hung the picture from one of the clothespins. "The first pic of the day."

He wasn't expecting her to whirl around so quickly. His hands shot out to steady her. The firmness of her upper arms under his palms short-circuited his brain. The moment froze, and instead of dropping his hands like any normal human being would, he let his palms travel down the soft material of the thin sweater that covered her arms.

Her eyes grew wide. Excitement flared in them. He pressed closer so they were a whisker away from their bodies touching.

"You have all this energy." His voice was husky as he tenderly touched her cheek. "You make me feel alive."

"I do?" Her big brown eyes blinked up at him, and he noted that she leaned toward him, not away.

"Yeah. I mean, you get things done. You juggle a lot of responsibilities. How do you do it?" He took a small section of her hair and let his fingers slide through it. Soft. Silky.

"I don't know." She shrugged, not tearing her gaze from his. "It all needs to be done, so I do it."

The air shimmered with more than sugarplums and dreams of Santa. The only thing he wanted to do was kiss her, but reason overrode the desire.

"I think I've been alone too long," he said softly, letting his hand drop.

A shadow crossed her face, but then she nodded with a sad smile. "I think I have been, too."

He prepared to step back, but to his surprise, she reached up and kissed his cheek. The softness of her lips on his skin rooted him to the spot, and it took every ounce of his willpower not to haul her in his arms and kiss her for real.

But he didn't. He couldn't. This was his boss. The woman who, through no fault of her own, was embroiled in his complicated custody arrangement. He had the sneaking suspicion he could find a way past their exes. And he could always get another job. But Erica herself?

He was growing too emotionally close to her.

As she brushed past him, he took a deep breath. *She's off-limits.* But as they continued making the rounds, he couldn't help but wonder what would it be like to kiss Erica Black. For real.

Could he make a woman like her happy? Or would he only disappoint her, too?

"Weindeer, Mommy!"

"Okay, okay." Erica's shoulders ached as Rowan stared up at her with his arms wrapped around her leg. The line for the reindeer had been too long earlier, but as the afternoon wore on, the crowds were thinning out. "Let's go feed those reindeer."

"With Gwady." He loosened his hold on her leg to put his hands together as if praying. "Pwease?"

Her smile froze in place. Grady. And Dalton. The four of them kept running into each other as they enjoyed the Christmas festival, and every time they did, she'd feel her neck warm. What had she been thinking this morning? Kissing Dalton? Even if it was only on the cheek?

"Sure, baby. Do you see him?" She held Rowan's hand as they looked around the children's craft area, where they'd been for the past half hour.

When they first arrived, Rowan had picked out frosted sugar cookies in the shape of snowmen from the bake sale, and Erica had added them to the pumpkin rolls she absolutely could not pass up. Then they'd purchased a few new ornaments for their Christmas tree. Taken Rowan's picture with Santa. And made their way around the craft area with hot chocolates and popcorn.

Every time she'd spotted Dalton, she couldn't help comparing him to her brothers. He was a doting father, like Jet and Blaine both were. While Jamie loved Rowan, he didn't have the patience to help him squirt glitter glue on a star ornament or play beanbag toss with him the way Dalton had with Grady.

Maybe she wasn't being fair. Who knew what Jamie did during their weekends together? He might have been a lousy husband, but he seemed to be a good father.

"I see him! Gwady!" Rowan pointed to the popcorn stand, where Dalton was handing a white bag to his son.

He almost took off, but she kept a firm grip on his hand and navigated a sea of children and parents as they began heading that way. Several people stopped her to rave about the pole barn and thank her for hosting the festival. The compliments warmed her heart, and she made sure to give the credit to all the people who'd worked so hard to put the event together.

Finally, they reached the table where Grady and Dalton had taken their snacks.

"So…" Just looking at Dalton made her heart go pitter-patter. "Are you two up for feeding some reindeer with us?"

"Yes!" Grady pumped both fists in the air and turned to his dad. "Can we, Daddy?"

"Of course." Dalton gave her a fleeting, but warm, glance and turned to Rowan. "Do you think any of them are Santa's reindeer?"

"Yeah." Rowan's eyes grew round with excitement. "Santa's weindeer."

"Come on!" Grady had climbed off the chair and was pulling on Dalton's hand to stand up, which he did with a laugh.

"We need to get our coats on first." Erica picked up Rowan and settled him on her hip. Dalton hoisted Grady onto his shoulders. They walked together to the coat table near the entrance. She smiled up at Grady. "Are you having fun?"

"Yes! I made a baby Jesus ornament. He's in the cradle because there was no room in the inn." Grady gave her a toothy grin as he wrapped his hands under Dalton's chin. "Right, Daddy?"

"That's right." His low voice sent a surge of warmth to her toes, as did the fact that he was sharing the gospel with his son.

"I made a snowman." Rowan twisted in her arms to face Grady. "Baby Jesus did, too."

Dalton met her eyes, and she couldn't help chuckling.

"Sorry, but no, Rowan," she said. "Baby Jesus didn't actually make a snowman."

"He didn't?" His little face looked heartbroken.

"No, but He *was* born in a stable, and that's where animals are kept. We're going to pet the little lambs and bunnies and goats after we see the reindeer."

"Yay!"

The next ten minutes were spent getting coats zipped and hats on, then racing out to get in the back of the line for the reindeer.

The boys were giggling and craning their necks every few seconds to see if it was their turn yet. Erica and Dalton stood behind them.

"Having fun?" he asked her.

She nodded, grinning. "Oh, yeah. It's been even better than I imagined. Can you get over how many people showed up?"

"The turnout is pretty incredible." He shoved one hand in his pocket and the other was inches from Grady's shoulder. "Putting out the jar for donations for the community center was smart."

"You know how people are—they want to help and don't always know how." She shrugged. "Plus, Clem volunteered to be in charge of it. He's been watching the jar like a hawk."

"I'm surprised he hasn't frightened people away."

"Or scared them into giving more." She laughed at the thought. Dalton did, too.

Slowly, the line inched forward.

"These two are going to be exhausted tonight." Dalton's tender smile as he stared at the boys made her stomach flip.

She'd spent enough time with him to respect his cowboy and leadership skills. And the time they'd spent working on this festival—as well as off-duty—made her equally impressed with him as a man. But this, seeing him with his son—it was turning her heart to mush.

He was a caring, attentive father.

And she realized what Rowan was missing by only spending every other weekend with Jamie. A part-time dad wasn't enough for her little boy. And there wasn't much she could do about it.

Regrets practically choked her. She hated that her son was missing out on having his mom and dad together full-time. She hated that Jamie had thrown away their life together for Haley.

"You two are next." A cute girl in her late teens held the gate closed and addressed the boys. "You have to hold your mommy or daddy's hand the whole time you're in there, okay?"

They looked up at her and nodded. The girl began reciting the rules and finally asked if they planned on feeding the reindeer.

Dalton paid for food for both boys. "Keep the change."

Soon they were inside the pen. Erica held Rowan's hand, while Dalton held Grady's. The boys each carried a small plastic container of reindeer food. The deer gravitated their way.

"Look, Mama!" Rowan tried to point at the reindeer and spilled half of his food. "Oh, no, I dwopped it!"

"It's okay, baby." She crouched, expecting him to start wailing. "Hold the dish out straight. There's plenty in there for him to eat."

With his little lips pouting and tears in the corner of his eyes, Rowan held out the dish, and to his delight, the deer ate all the food in it. Then Erica lifted him so he could pet the reindeer.

"Rowan, I think that one's Rudolph!" Grady zoomed over to them, with Dalton by his side.

The boys pet all three reindeer, and Erica asked Dalton to stay close to Rowan so she could take a few pictures. Her favorite was of Dalton crouching with his arms around each boy while one of the bucks stared directly into the camera. Then Dalton got a few pictures of her with the boys and the reindeer.

When their time was up, Erica helped corral the boys back out of the pen. "Think they can handle petting the lambs? Or would it be too much fun for one day?"

"Are you kidding?" Dalton grinned. They boys raced ahead to the tent. "I've been waiting for hours to hold a bunny."

She pointed to the entrance. "Well, your wish is about to come true."

Over the next twenty minutes, the boys laughed at the baby goats kicking up their hind legs, and they tentatively petted the lambs. Then they ended up sitting next to each other on hay bales with bunnies on their laps.

Erica took picture after picture, including several of Dalton holding a fluffy gray rabbit.

"Why don't I get a picture of the four of you?" Christy Moulten appeared by her side. Erica hadn't even noticed her come into the tent. "The boys look so cute together. They could be brothers."

"That's because they are. Stepbrothers." Erica looked at them fondly. They were petting each other's bunnies.

"All the more reason to get a picture of you all. Go on." Christy plucked Erica's phone out of her hand and waved them to move together. "Don't be shy."

"Oh, um…" Dalton handed Erica the gray bunny and rubbed his chin. "I'll sit this one out. You get in there."

"Nonsense, Dalton." Christy took a step closer and pointed for him to move behind the boys. "Erica, you get back there, too."

Erica cradled the calm bunny and tried to decide if it was worth protesting. Maybe it would be better to take the picture and get it over with. Christy wasn't one to change her mind.

"Oh, almost got it." Christy lifted her chin. "Can you stand a wee bit closer?"

Erica was certain her cheeks must be flaming redder than Santa's suit at this point.

"Boys, give me a big smile and say 'bunnies,' okay?"

"Bunnies!" they shouted.

As soon as Christy finished taking the pictures, she handed the phone back and sat on a hay bale, asking Rowan and Grady about the fun they'd had today. They answered all her questions and insisted she pet each of their bunnies.

Erica carried the gray one over to the handler and Dalton joined her. She glanced up at him. "Sorry about that."

"Don't be." He shook his head and there was something vulnerable and poignant in his expression. It was as if he felt it, too—the sadness of a broken family—but also the joy of an almost family to share these moments. "It's been a special day. The picture will be a reminder of it. A good memory."

"What a nice thought. I'll text you the pics later." She squirted hand sanitizer on her palms and rubbed them together. Christy was still in deep, animated conversation with the boys. "I'm so glad we have plenty of volunteers to take everything down tonight. After all the work we did setting it up…"

"Yeah, I know." He rubbed hand sanitizer on his hands, too. "And whatever isn't taken care of tonight, we can deal with later this week."

She smiled. "You're right."

"Have you ever thought about making the pole barn into an event center?"

"An event center?" She frowned and moved to the side to allow two middle school girls to pass by.

"Yeah. You're a natural at planning things."

They stepped around the bales on their way back to the boys. "But the community center's roof will be fixed by summer."

Christy shifted her attention to them. "What's this about the community center?"

"I mentioned the pole barn would make a good event center," Dalton said.

"An event center?" The older woman's face lit up and she rose from her seat. "Yes! That's exactly what we need." She stepped toward Erica and hooked arms with her. "Think of all the weddings you could host."

"But the community center—"

"Is too small." Christy patted her arm, which was still wound in hers. "For intimate weddings, it's fine. But your barn could host a much larger crowd."

She opened her mouth to protest, but then closed it. Why was she protesting? The idea took root, then started fizzing in her heart. Soon her entire chest was ready to burst with excitement. Why couldn't she make the pole barn into an event center?

"Do you think Jewel River needs it?" She looked from Dalton to Christy. They both nodded. Then Christy started listing all of the other events it could house, including family reunions and community events like this one.

"Mama?" Rowan wrapped his arm around her leg and rubbed his eyes with his other hand.

"Oh, my, you look tired." She picked him up and kissed his cheek. "Where's your bunny?"

He pointed to a boy and a girl who were now holding his and Grady's rabbits.

"I think we need to call it quits for the day." Erica caressed his hair. "Let's get some sanitizer on those hands."

"Us, too." Dalton picked up Grady, who was also yawning.

"Call me." Christy tapped her phone. "We can talk it over more. And you go home and rest. The festival will be over in an hour. I'll talk to the cleanup crew. We can take over from here."

"Thanks, Christy. I really appreciate it."

The woman said goodbye to the boys and to Dalton. Then they got the boys to rub sanitizer on their hands.

"I'm taking him back home," Erica said as they left the tent. "Thanks for a great day. I'll text you those pictures later."

"I appreciate it." They continued through the parking

lot on their way to the drive leading to her house. "Maybe I'll see you in church tomorrow."

"You will." Her mouth opened wide in a yawn. She was as tired as Rowan. "See you tomorrow."

He nudged his chin up, his eyes smoldering. And as the hunky cowboy kept walking with his son on his hip, Erica couldn't help wishing he wasn't heading to his cabin, that he and Grady would spend the evening with her and Rowan.

But they'd spent enough time together as it was. Time to go home and get back to reality.

Chapter Ten

He couldn't get Erica off his mind.

Dalton shoved a coil of barbed-wire fencing on the shelf in the storage shed almost two weeks later on Thursday afternoon. He and Lars had repaired a section of fence in the bulls' pasture, and he was still trying to get feeling back into his frozen fingers. The weather gave new meaning to the Christmas song trapped in his head, "Baby It's Cold Outside." It certainly was. The song had him picturing Erica sipping cocoa in front of the Christmas tree, laughing with him, enjoying the holidays together.

Which wasn't going to happen.

Maybe it was just wishful thinking, since he'd agreed to watch a Christmas movie with her and Gemma at her place tonight. Gemma had refused to take payment for watching Grady before the festival. She'd said she wanted the three of them to watch one of those Hallmark movies. He couldn't turn her down…even if he'd wanted to.

He straightened the shelves and kept an eye out for anything that needed to be reordered. Christmas Eve was this Sunday already, and he was having regrets about the custody schedule he'd worked out with Haley. He wouldn't see Grady at all on Christmas Eve, and he wouldn't pick the boy up until Monday, Christmas Day, at ten in the morning. Since Dalton would be missing both Christmas Eve and the Christmas morning wake-up, Haley agreed he could keep Grady two extra days.

It had seemed a good compromise at the time, but, as usual, he reckoned he'd gotten the short end of the stick.

With a huff, he finished up in the storage room and rubbed his hands on his way to the office. Erica would be there in half an hour, and he needed to go over the feedlot numbers before she arrived. He promptly took a seat and turned on the heater.

"Anything else you need me to do, boss?" Sam paused in the doorway with his hands on either side of the frame.

"You broke the ice again, right?" The cows were in a pasture with a creek that needed to have the ice broken in order for them to drink.

"Just got back from doing it."

"Then I'll see you tomorrow."

"See ya."

After checking his phone quickly—no texts—he reviewed what he needed to do before Christmas.

He'd bought Grady's presents. Still needed to wrap them. He'd ordered his gift for Erica. She'd given him a new beginning here, and every single day, he practically jumped out of bed with a renewed zest for life. Sugarpie was thriving here, too. All because of her.

He'd ordered her a large, soft scarf that seemed to be more of a shawl, as well as an intricate glass ornament in the shape of a snowflake. It was supposed to arrive today.

His phone rang. Haley. Hmm. She usually texted him. Was Grady okay?

"What's up?" he asked.

"Hi, Dalton." Her breathy voice made his stomach clench. "I want to run something by you."

"What is it?" And how much was it going to cost him?

"Jamie and I are taking the boys to a movie Saturday, and since he's picking up Rowan, why don't I ride with him so you can see Grady for a few minutes?"

The thought of seeing Grady—even for a few minutes—tempted him. But not if it meant having Jamie around and watching Haley play the devoted wife to anyone but him.

"No. We already worked this out."

"So you'd rather not see your son at all before Christmas? Why? To punish me?"

"I'm not punishing you. We have an agreement. I don't see the point in changing it."

"You're so stubborn."

He wasn't even responding to that. Everything about this conversation was simmering his blood to a boil.

"Fine, I'll tell Grady his daddy doesn't want to see him."

"Don't use him against me." He couldn't believe her nerve. "Is that what you do? Tell my son lies behind my back?"

"I don't know what you're talking about."

"Why would you ever tell him I don't want to see him?" He reached for a pen, then began clicking it open and shut. *Click, click.* "You know I want to see him every minute I can. I wouldn't do that to you. This has nothing to do with him, and you know it."

"You hate me so much I can't even bring our son over?" Her whisper voice made him click the pen even faster.

He was not getting pulled into her guilt trip. Not this time.

"You left me, Haley. You left me." *Click, click, click.*

"So you *are* punishing me."

"Look, I'm busy. I'll pick Grady up Christmas Day like we planned. Gotta go." Before he had to listen to one more word in her barely there voice, he ended the call.

Not his finest moment. And he'd had a lot of bad moments over the past two years. Would this ever get better?

He had years and years of awkward encounters with her and Jamie to look forward to. School events. Sports. Graduation.

He covered his head with his hands.

Was he ever going to stop resenting her new husband? Was he ever going to feel like anything but a failure when dealing with them?

"Knock, knock," Erica said in a singsong voice in the doorway. He jerked to attention, waving her to come in and sit down, which she did. "Gemma is arranging a platterful of cookies for tonight as we speak. My mouth is watering just thinking about them. I can't believe you agreed to the movie. Wait…what's wrong?"

She stripped off her gloves and set them on the desk. Her cheeks were pink from the cold.

"Nothing."

She tilted her head, giving him a blank look.

"Haley called." He shouldn't have admitted it. Should pretend everything was fine and that his ex-wife didn't still tie him into knots.

"What did she want?"

Belatedly, he realized Haley's suggestion would bother Erica, and the last thing she needed was to worry about Jamie bringing Haley with him to pick up Rowan on Saturday. "Just hashing out the holiday schedule."

"I'm dreading it." Her face cleared in sympathy. "Never

in my wildest dreams did I think I'd be spending every other Christmas without my son. And he's at the fun age, you know? When Christmas morning is all dreamy and special."

"Yeah, I know." Dalton leaned back, nodding thoughtfully. "I feel the same."

"One thing this holiday has forced me to do is rethink my future."

"What do you mean?"

"I guess it's hard letting go of the imaginary future I had in my head when I married Jamie and then had Rowan. I pictured years of special Christmas mornings together. If anyone had told me then what my life would be like now?" She shook her head. "I wouldn't have believed them."

"Would you have done anything differently?" He asked himself the question often, but he never sat with it long enough to come up with an answer.

"I don't know." She shrugged, looking sad. "It doesn't really matter. Can't change it. The only thing I can do is move forward. What about you?"

He opened his mouth to reply, then closed it. He still hadn't sat with it long enough to come up with an answer.

"I don't know, either. I'm a grown man, but I'm not sure who I was when I was married, and I don't always know who I am now."

"Well, I didn't know you then, but I know you now. You're a good man, Dalton. Someone I can rely on. Not only me, but everyone on this ranch. The other employees, the cattle, even Gemma. We're glad you're here."

Unexpected emotions pressed against his chest. Appreciation wasn't something he had much experience with.

His grandparents had loved him and raised him, but

they'd made it clear ranching was his duty. Haley had loved him and married him, but she'd made it clear he wasn't holding up his end of her marriage expectations.

No matter how hard he'd worked, how much he'd given, it had never been appreciated.

Until now.

As he stared at the outgoing woman who always had a kind word to say, something shifted inside him.

"That means a lot to me, Erica." He enjoyed the way her name felt rolling off his tongue. "Your great-aunt and uncle left the ranch in good hands when they gave it to you. You're a good boss. And a good mom."

A blush crept to her cheeks. "I don't know about that."

"I do. You're special. I've never met anyone like you. You're a good friend, too."

Her eyelashes started fluttering like butterfly wings, and he ran a finger under his collar. What had gotten into him? He wasn't one to throw out compliments like that.

But Erica really was special.

She was nothing like his ex-wife, that was for sure. Erica was direct and took responsibility. She shouldered burdens many would throw up their hands in surrender to.

"Can I ask you a question?" he asked.

"Go for it."

"When did you know you were over Jamie?"

Her mouth formed an O, and she blew out an exhalation. "That's a tough one. You couldn't have asked me something easy like what to buy Grady for Christmas?"

"You're right," he said. "Too personal. Forget it."

"No, no." She raised her palms. "I'll answer."

It took her several moments before she continued. "I didn't know it at the time, but I think I was over him the moment I decided to ask you to manage the ranch. Before then, I was too upset about the divorce to consider anything that would have brought our two families closer together…for any reason. And, well, don't judge me, but Haley is stunningly beautiful, and Jamie obviously preferred her to me, so…" She looked up at the ceiling. "I'm over him, but I might not ever get over his betrayal. It messes with me. Still."

Dalton sat back, surprised. "You don't know how pretty you are, do you?"

There went her eyelashes again. And her expression was like an animal freezing in its tracks.

"Jamie was a fool to ever let you go."

"Like Haley wasn't a fool to give you up?"

"She got the better end of the deal by leaving me." It was freeing to finally admit it. "I could never give her what she wanted. My ranch was not a moneymaker. We had enough to pay the bills and not much extra."

"I didn't marry Jamie for money." Erica leaned in. "She didn't marry you for it, either."

"Trust me, I know." He'd laugh if it wasn't so pathetic.

"She gave up a man with integrity—you—for a man who puts himself first. Dumb move."

"Integrity is good and all, but deep down, I don't really blame Haley for wanting more." He rubbed his chin, feeling more vulnerable than he could ever remember. "No offense, but you're not poor. And I've been to your folks' house. They aren't poor, either. You don't know what it's like. The reality is I couldn't afford to give Haley much other than a ten-year-old minivan and a run-down house."

"You're right. I'm not poor. I've never known what it's like to struggle financially." Her face grew more animated as she talked. "But I know why I got married, and it wasn't for things Jamie could buy me. I wanted a partner. A man to raise a family with. A man I could count on. All the money in the world can't buy that. Give yourself a little more credit."

Give himself more credit? More? When he'd never given himself any to begin with?

"I'll do that on one condition." He watched her intently.

"What is it?"

"You have to give yourself more credit, too." His voice turned gruff. "You deserve a man you can count on."

Her sharp intake of breath told him he'd caught her off-guard.

"And you deserve someone who appreciates you," she said.

When Erica looked at him like that, he believed her. And he finally conceded that maybe she was right. Maybe he had more to offer than he'd given himself credit for. Maybe he had more to offer a woman than he thought.

"Have another cookie, Daltie." Gemma brought the platter over to the corner of the sectional where Dalton was sitting. Erica was curled up at the other end. Her lips twitched in mirth whenever Gemma used her nickname for Dalton. The woman positively doted on the man.

"Uh, thanks, Gemma." He selected a gingerbread man with icing. "You know, this movie isn't too bad."

"Not too bad? It's wonderful." Gemma set the platter back on the coffee table. Clutching two thumbprint cookies, she sat back in her chair. She had a jingle-bell barrette in her hair that tinkled every time she moved. Plus, she was wearing a red Christmas sweatshirt with two kittens in Santa hats. If Rowan was awake, he would have loved it. Erica had put him to bed shortly before Gemma and

Dalton arrived for the movie, though. Gemma nibbled on a cookie. "I just know he's going to realize his secret Santa is her, and he's going to feel like such a dummy when he does."

Erica took another sip of her decaf coffee and eyed the double chocolate chip cookies. She'd already had three. Would one more really hurt? It was the holidays, after all. She plucked another one off the platter and took a bite. Yum.

"I think we should wear matching shirts next year. To watch our movie. What do you think?" Gemma nodded to herself, then smiled at them both. "Isn't this fun?"

Erica bit her lip to keep from laughing. Matching shirts? Only Gemma would be comfortable throwing that idea out there with a rugged manly man in the room.

The living room was filled with Christmas spirit, and it wasn't the twinkly decorations, the sugary-sweet romantic movie on television or the cookies they were munching on. It was the company. Gemma, who saw the best in people and went out of her way to make them feel good, and Dalton, who looked as out of place watching a Hallmark movie as a cowboy could in his flannel shirt and jeans, yet somehow appeared to be right at home here.

Last year at this time, Erica had never felt lonelier, even with Great-Aunt Martha a room away and having Gemma down the lane. But this year? It felt like home.

"What kind of shirts are you thinking?" Dalton's low voice made Erica let out a tiny sigh. He was kind. And he liked Gemma. And the genuine curiosity in his question made Erica want to go over and hug him.

Bless that man for not making fun of her sweet housekeeper and for joining them tonight.

"It should have something to do with our Christmas movies. And, you know, I've always loved Yorkies."

"The dogs?" he asked. She smiled and nodded.

"How about 'I bark for Christmas movies' with a Yorkie's face under it?" Erica was only half-serious as she threw out the suggestion.

"See?" Gemma pointed to her. "You are so smart, Erica. It's the perfect shirt."

Erica caught Dalton's eye. "What do you think, Daltie? Matching shirts for next year?"

"Sure, why not?" He gave her a weak smile. And she gave him a toothy grin in response. Then his expression grew flirtatious with a spark of challenge. "I'll even have them made."

"Oh, you will?" She kept the sarcasm light as her pulse began to speed up. "Thanks, Big D."

"Yep." He turned to Gemma. "What color do you like best?"

"Red would give it the holiday spirit, don't you think?"

"Yes, I do." He nodded. "Ladies, you tell me the sizes to order, and I'll take care of it."

"Wonderful!" Gemma beamed, brushing the crumbs off her lap. "Just think how much fun we'll have next year. If only it wasn't so far away."

"Well, we still have tonight," Erica reminded her, then pointed to the television. "Look, it's back on."

The movie continued, and Gemma was correct—the woman did turn out to be the guy's secret Santa. By the time they kissed at the end, Erica had a feeling she looked as dreamy-eyed as Gemma over there. She stole a glance at Dalton, who was staring at her. He quickly averted his gaze.

Their conversation in the ranch office earlier came

back to her. She'd thought about it off and on all evening. It wasn't like her to have revealing conversations with anyone about her marriage. Why Dalton made her want to let down her walls, she couldn't say, but he did. And she was glad he did, because it had given her clarity on a few things.

One, she truly was over Jamie. Her reaction to his childish need to bend their custody rules wasn't based on any lingering love for the man. She merely wanted him to suffer the consequences of his actions. Not that he ever would.

Two, she had a better understanding of Dalton and what had gone wrong in his marriage. And she ached for him. Wanted to wrap him in her arms, look him in the eye and tell him he was so much more than he thought. That he was ten times the man Jamie ever could be. That, rich or poor, she'd want him by her side any day over her selfish ex. Not that she ever would.

And three, her heart was in the danger zone. It had been for a while. Her attraction had kicked up to an entirely new level at the Christmas festival, and it was getting worse each day.

"Well, kids, I'm headed home." Pushing off the chair's arms, Gemma stood up. "It was a fun night."

Dalton stood, too, and thanked her for the cookies. Erica followed them both down the hall.

"I'll walk you home," he said as Gemma put her coat on.

"That's okay, Daltie." She patted his arm. "The moon is shining tonight and the wind's died down. I like to be alone with my thoughts on a night like this."

"Are you sure?" he asked.

"I'm sure." Then she gathered her things and hugged

them both before walking outside on the porch. "See you tomorrow."

Once Gemma was safely on the sidewalk, Erica shut the door.

"I should probably go, too." Dalton stood under the chandelier and showed no signs of wanting to leave. Erica took it as a good sign.

"Nah, it's early." She waved him to follow her and padded back down the hall to the living room. "You haven't told me what you got Grady for Christmas."

She sensed him behind her and was surprised at how glad she was he didn't fight her on staying. She settled back into the corner of the sectional, curling her legs under her body. Dalton sat a few feet away.

"I got him a kiddie workbench and a plastic tool set— the drill spins and everything—and a stuffed lion. A couple of books. What about you?"

"A tricycle. I think Rowan will have fun with it." She bit her lower lip. "I got him books, too, and more toy cars. He loves them."

"Yeah, Grady loves them, too."

Was she imagining the simmering connection they had? It took all of her willpower not to uncurl her legs and scoot right next to him.

"Did you ask Santa for anything?" he asked, his eyes laughing.

"Santa gave me an early present. The best ranch manager I could ask for."

His gaze sharpened, then mellowed.

"What else was on the list?" He leaned closer to her, making her pulse go faster.

She shrugged, hoping he'd reach out and touch her—

hold her hand, put his arm around her shoulder...anything, really.

"Nothing money can buy." Had she said that out loud?

His thigh bumped into her knee, and she uncurled her legs, feeling as wide-eyed and full of anticipation as she'd been in high school when she'd gotten her first kiss.

"Like what?" His cologne was killing her. Reminded her of the ocean. Made her want to inhale it for hours.

Maybe now was as good a time as any to be honest about what she wanted—really wanted—out of life.

"I want a family."

He looked perplexed. "You have one."

"I'm not talking about my parents and siblings. I'm not even talking about Rowan." She licked her lips, unsure if she should say the things so deep in her heart. "I want to have a husband. I want more children."

There. She'd admitted it. Out loud.

Her face burned, and she couldn't bear to look at him. Didn't want to see pity or something worse.

To her surprise, he put his finger on her chin and turned her to face him. She didn't see pity. Or anything worse.

"I want more kids, too." His face was close to hers, and she probed his eyes, desperate to make sure he wasn't lying to her—not that he'd ever lied to her. But this... It was too important not to verify. Jamie had told her things she'd wanted to hear. Then, when she called him out on it, he'd backed off, claiming he'd never said them in the first place.

But whatever was in Dalton's eyes convinced her he was speaking the truth.

"What about a wife?" she asked.

His eyelashes lowered momentarily. "I wouldn't have more kids without a wife."

"You wouldn't get married just to have kids, would you?" Disappointment pressed against her heart.

"No…" He shook his head. "That came out wrong. I…" His shoulders slumped. "I don't think I could handle another divorce."

Ahh. She understood. "I know what you mean. I don't think I could, either."

"But I'd be lying if I said you didn't tempt me." Dalton reached over and twined a tendril of her hair around his finger. She savored the feeling of holding a man's attention. It had been so long since she'd felt like she was anything beyond a mother or a boss.

Dalton wasn't just any man.

She pressed a teensy bit closer to him.

"Erica," he said in a gravelly voice, "I, that is, we shouldn't…"

"Shouldn't what?" She cupped his cheek with her hand and stared into his eyes. There was no denying the truth in them—he was attracted to her. Wanted to kiss her. As badly as she wanted to kiss him.

"You're my boss."

"I don't think of you as an employee."

"Then how do you think of me?" His gaze was glued to her lips.

"I think of you as a man. A good man."

That was all it took. He wrapped his hand behind her neck and leaned closer. She closed her eyes and when his mouth pressed against hers, she sighed, sliding her arms around his neck. He kissed her slowly, thoroughly, like a man who'd been eyeing a pitcher of ice water after a long day riding in the sun.

She poured her emotions into the kiss. He made her feel powerful and weak at the same time—which made no sense. He tasted like cookies, and he was careful with her. Oh, so careful.

This was a man who could make her fall so hard for him, she'd never recover if he left her. She pulled away from the kiss, forced herself to disengage from his touch.

"I'm… That is, I…" Her lips felt swollen, and her thoughts hadn't been this scattered in years. Maybe ever.

He looked just as shell-shocked as she was as he drew back, raking his hand through his hair. "I know. I shouldn't have. I'll—I'll just go."

"You don't have to—" But he was already on his feet and on his way down the hall. She rushed after him.

"I'm sorry." He bent over and pulled a cowboy boot over his foot as he stared up at her. "It was unprofessional and wrong and I need this job and…"

"It's not like I'm going to fire you," she huffed, putting a hand on her hip.

"I wouldn't blame you if you did." He hauled the other boot on and stood in front of her. All she could do was stare at his chest and try not to think about touching him again.

"We're not little kids, Dalton. I'm attracted to you. You're attracted to me. We'll handle it."

He shoved one arm into his jacket and reached for the door. "It won't happen again."

As he hurried outside, she called after him, "What if I want it to? Don't I have any say?"

He stopped on the sidewalk and turned back to her. "You're right that we aren't little kids, Erica. These are grown-up games, ones I shouldn't be playing. Good night."

And with that, he strode away, leaving her freezing in the doorway, unsure of what had just happened.

As much as she wanted to go after him and tell him he was wrong, she couldn't.

Because deep down, Erica knew he was right.

Chapter Eleven

Dalton was proud of himself. He'd managed to pretend the kiss the other night never happened…at least when he was around Erica. But the rest of the time?

He couldn't stop thinking about her. About how she made him feel. About how this ranch was the best thing that had happened to him in years. About how much he wanted to kiss her again.

"I'd better get back to the house. Jamie's picking up Rowan in an hour." Erica strode next to him as they headed from the ranch office to the main driveway on Saturday morning. A light snow fell, and she held out her gloved hands and tilted her head to look up at the sky. "Maybe we'll have a white Christmas, after all."

"I hope so." A bubble of joy surrounded her. He wanted to reach out and touch it.

She gave him a sideways glance. "I'm nervous about spending tomorrow without Rowan."

"Yeah, I know the feeling."

"What are you going to do? Special Christmas Eve plans?"

"Tomorrow?" He looked back over his shoulder. "Check

cattle. Do a few chores. I told Lars and Sam they could have the day off. What about you?"

"Gemma and I are making sticky buns in the morning. I'll head to church later. I keep trying to get her to join me, but she said she'll watch the service online."

"If you get bored, you can always ride out and check cattle with me." Why had he suggested that? *Dumb. You like being with her. You want to spend every minute you can with her. Admit it.*

"Checking cattle in the freezing cold? I'll pass, although it would definitely take my mind off Rowan." The sparkle in her eyes mesmerized him. He forced himself to look away.

They passed the equipment shed and came to the fork in the road where they always parted. The lane leading to the cabins was to the right, and the path to her house was to the left.

"Oh, I almost forgot," she said. "Gemma left you a plate of cookies on the counter. Shortbread, snickerdoodles and chocolate chip, from the looks of it. You can pick it up now, if you'd like. I have no idea why she leaves food for you at my house when you're practically next door to her, but I've stopped asking myself questions about Gemma's way of doing things."

He chuckled, joining her on the path to the left. "I'm not passing up her cookies."

"I wouldn't, either." The snow continued to fall as they strolled.

"What do you think about painting the old barn over on the south side of the ranch next summer?" he asked. It was one of the few buildings that was showing signs of wear and tear. "We'd have to do a few repairs first."

"I hadn't thought about it, but now that you mention it,

I think it's smart. You know, I've always had a thing for red barns."

They chatted until they reached her side yard. Then Erica came to a dead stop.

And he did, too.

In the driveway up ahead, Jamie and Haley were getting out of an expensive SUV. Haley opened the door to the back seat and unstrapped Grady before lifting him out and setting him on the ground. The boy spotted Dalton, then yelled, "Daddy!" and ran to him.

Dalton's brain ground to a halt. Sure, his body welcomed the boy into his arms. But he couldn't comprehend the sight in front of him.

Haley. Here. With Jamie. In violation of their custody arrangement.

The day before Christmas Eve.

What was she thinking?

"What do you think you're doing?" Erica said, practically hissing at Jamie. Her normally animated face was pale, her tone icy.

"Hey, Grady," Dalton said, picking him up, "why don't you say hi to Rowan for a minute?" He carried him away from the crime scene, and moments later, opened the front door and called out, "Gemma, Grady's here. Can he hang out with you guys for a few minutes?"

"Of course, Daltie," she said. "Come on back here, Grady. We're playing with stickers."

Grady raced down the hall, and Dalton headed back outside, down the steps to stand next to Erica. The conversation had already grown tense.

"…a blatant disregard for the legal arrangements we made." Erica's color had returned. Dalton glanced at Jamie and wanted to wipe the smug look off his face.

"You're being obnoxious." Jamie stared down his nose at her. "We have plans and don't have time for me to pick up Rowan and then drive all the way home to get Haley and Grady."

"I don't really care what your plans are. You could have dropped them off anywhere in Jewel River, but you didn't. You're an hour early, and you're supposed to be alone." Her arms were down by her sides, her hands balled into fists. She stood tall. Unwavering.

Dalton had never been more impressed by her.

He moved over to Haley. "What are you doing here? I thought we went over this on the phone."

"I don't know why you insist on punishing me." Her pale blue eyes grew watery as she stared at him.

"I'm not punishing you." He turned away, refusing to engage in her martyr act. He'd put up with it since he was in high school, and he couldn't do it another minute.

"Lighten up," Jamie said to Erica. "I don't need a lecture from you."

"And I don't need your lame excuses. You think you can do whatever you want…"

"See what he has to put up with?" Haley said to Dalton, jerking her head their way. "The hoops he has to jump through?"

"Are you kidding me?" Dalton stepped back, grimacing. Her perception of the situation astounded him. "This isn't what we agreed on. It's not that hard to follow a schedule."

"Of course, you'd take her side." Haley sniffed. "I have to be the villain."

He wanted to shout, "You are the villain! You two are the villains."

"What did she just say?" Erica, glaring at Jamie, turned

her attention to Haley. "You have no right to be here, let alone commentate on the situation."

"She's my wife." Jamie moved over to Haley and put his arm around her shoulders.

Dalton clenched his jaw. The perfect couple. Here. The day before Christmas Eve. Rubbing it in his face and Erica's.

"She has no right to be here," Erica said.

"She has every right to be here." Jamie narrowed his eyes. "Stop being such a drama queen."

Erica looked like she'd been slapped.

"Hold it right there." Dalton raised his right hand, palm out, and glared at Jamie. "You're wrong."

"I didn't ask for your opinion," Jamie scoffed. "Stay in your lane."

"I told you he wouldn't be reasonable." Haley cuddled into Jamie's side like a wounded animal.

Anger burned in Dalton's gut. All the times Haley and Jamie had looked down on him. All the times she'd treated him like he was her personal ATM machine. All the times they'd acted like he was some dumb hick. They all roared back.

This—this display a couple days before Christmas—was the final straw.

"What do you want?" Dalton said to Haley. "What are you trying to prove? You cheated on me. Not the other way around. And now you've got everything you ever wanted. A new husband, a new house, his money, *my* money. You've got our son full-time. What more can you possibly want from me?"

Haley glanced at Jamie. "I told you he's only working here to punish me."

"He's working here," Erica said as she took a step toward them, "because he's the best ranch manager in the county. It has nothing to do with you."

Jamie rolled his eyes. "He's working here because you're so petty, you think it would actually bother me. You're so predictable."

Dalton wanted to shout a dozen awful things to his ex-wife and her husband, but he could yell at them until he passed out, and they still wouldn't listen to a word he said.

Right now, he just wanted them gone.

"Predictable? Petty?" Erica shook her head, steam practically pouring out of her ears. "You're the poster boy for both. You're in breach of our custody agreement. I'm calling my lawyer."

"Go ahead." Jamie unwrapped his arm from Haley and stepped forward. "By the way, I'm throwing away that stupid stuffed rabbit tonight. He's too old for it."

"You wouldn't dare." Erica looked ready to explode. "Don't even think about touching Bunny."

Dalton moved between them. Then he addressed Haley. "You need to leave. Now."

Haley glared at him.

Erica pushed Dalton's arm aside to get into Jamie's face. "You crossed a line."

"What line?" Jamie spread his arms out. "I don't see one."

"Come on," Dalton said as he took Erica's arm, "let's go inside and say goodbye to the boys."

Erica snatched her arm free, not taking her eyes off Jamie, and Dalton was surprised the guy hadn't been burned to a crisp. "I'm not done."

"You're done," Dalton said quietly.

Then she faced him, and he sucked in a breath at all

the pain in her eyes. "You don't get to tell me when I'm done. I decide." She jammed her thumb into her chest. "Me. Got it?"

Dalton clenched his jaw and gave her a nod. "Got it."

And he turned on his heel and walked away. To get his son and pack the boy off with his inconsiderate mother and her arrogant husband so they could spend Christmas Eve together while he spent the day alone.

None of them—not Haley, not Jamie and obviously not Erica—respected him. The past five minutes had just proven it.

This was why he never should have agreed to work here in the first place.

He'd always known their exes would catch up to them. And they'd always be part of their lives, no matter how much he tried to avoid them.

Working here had turned out to be a big mistake.

That had been the most humiliating scene of her life.

"Don't ever do that to me again." Erica stood shaking on the porch with Dalton as Jamie and Haley drove away with the boys. The crunching of the gravel under the tires grated on her already destroyed nerves.

Gemma had wisely gone back to her cabin while they said goodbye to the children. Erica kept flexing her fingers to stop the adrenaline surging through her veins, but it didn't work.

Dalton's harsh jawline and the way he held himself as rigid as an oak tree warned her she was picking the wrong fight.

But she was so upset. How could Jamie have ambushed her like that? Her ex-husband *knew* the rules. He'd signed legally binding documents. Yet, he'd flouted them as usual.

And to see him protecting Haley while basically calling Erica a vindictive shrew had pushed every button she possessed. No wonder she was falling apart.

"I don't need *anyone* telling me what to do." She hiked her chin and crossed her arms over her chest, willing him to say something. "He was never supposed to bring her here."

And right before Christmas, no less. After she'd accommodated the jerk about having Rowan through Christmas morning and everything.

Some of her tension began to unravel at Dalton's silence.

"I can fight my own battles," she said. The war inside her began to die down.

He faced her then, and what she saw in his eyes made her shrivel.

"I won't ever tell you what to do again." The pain in his expression pierced her conscience. He'd been hurt, too. And she'd caused some of it. "You're the boss, after all."

"I didn't mean it like that." Her shoulders softened, and it struck her that she was about to lose something precious if she couldn't get her temper under control.

"Yes, you did. You meant it exactly like that." He could have been made of stone. "For the record, the situation was escalating, and I was trying to neutralize it."

"They were wrong. They're selfish and entitled, and I wasn't putting up with it."

He seemed to be judging her, and must have found her lacking by the disappointment in his eyes. Nothing new. Jamie found her lacking, too. Her anger morphed to pain.

"Is this how it's always going to be?" he asked quietly.

"What do you mean?" She rubbed her forearms, her tone hard.

"He's not going to change, you know."

If she made Jamie see how wrong he was...

Erica cringed. Was Dalton right? If he was, then all her yelling wouldn't matter. Because her ex would still walk all over her.

"I think I've accepted the fact that Haley is who she is," he said. "As I'm sure you just saw, she doesn't listen to a word I say. I've always just been here for her convenience."

"She doesn't know what she's missing."

"Neither do you."

"That's not true, Dalton." Erica blinked rapidly, feeling as if she could be knocked over with a breath.

"He wanted you to fight, Erica, and you gave him exactly what he wanted."

Her temper sprang back to life. "What am I supposed to do? Smile sweetly and pack my son off with him and his wife whenever they feel like showing up? Should I throw myself on the gravel and let him drive over my body on the way out?"

"I didn't say that."

She shook her head as tears started to gather. "At least I'm willing to fight. Haley treated you like dirt, too."

"Leave her out of it."

"Why? Oh, that's right, because she's fragile. Look at those big blue eyes wrong, and she'll break. You're too afraid to stand up to her."

"I'm not afraid. I just don't see the point."

"Sure." She knew better. The Haleys of the world got exactly what they wanted and suffered no repercussions. If Erica was smart, she'd play the victim card, too. Then maybe she wouldn't lash out and act like a cornered animal every time Jamie crossed her.

"I don't know how to explain it." Dalton's tone changed from upset to resigned. "All I've ever done is disappoint her. I thought maybe…"

"Do you still love her? Do you want her back?" All her worst fears regarding Dalton finally marched up and faced her like a firing squad. And she realized—too late—that her temper had blinded her.

She might be furious with Jamie, but seeing Dalton with his ex-wife had brought out her insecurities. Erica's feelings for him had grown over the past weeks, grown to the point where he'd become important to her.

More than important.

She was falling for the cowboy.

"No…" He shook his head, looking so disappointed she wanted to cry. "I don't love her anymore. I don't want her back. I thought, well…it doesn't matter. I'd only disappoint you, too."

She sucked in a breath. *No, no, no.* This wasn't how it was supposed to go.

He gave her a sad smile. "Don't worry. I won't make it awkward. We'll do things your way. I'm good at following orders." And then he tipped his hat to her and turned to leave.

"Dalton, wait." She'd botched this, the same way she'd botched everything else today. "That's not what I want. You're more than my employee. You're important. Really important to me."

"Give it a few days. You'll see I'm not."

"You're wrong, Dalton. I—"

"Look, it's been a rough day. Let's go our separate

ways. Lick our wounds in private." He held up a hand and walked away.

She stood on the porch until he was no longer in view. Then the cold seeped into her bones, and she went inside, stripped off her coat and boots and walked to the living room.

She'd finally gotten her life together. Finally started to feel good about herself. And where had she ended up? Confused. Alone. And as miserable as she could ever remember.

As much as she wanted to convince Dalton he was wrong—that he could never disappoint her—she knew she had to start facing facts.

She was in no position to have a relationship with him until she dealt with her anger toward Jamie.

Dalton was right. Jamie wasn't going to change. Which meant she had to.

And she didn't know if she had it in her.

Chapter Twelve

What a thickheaded fool he was.

Later that night, Dalton reclined on his couch and flipped through the channels. He'd been trying to avoid looking at the Christmas tree, mainly because every time he glanced at it he saw all of the ornaments Erica had generously given him. They told a different story about her than the one he'd written today.

He'd lumped her in with Haley when he'd declared he'd only disappoint her, too. That wasn't fair.

He'd judged her for boldly standing up to Jamie. That wasn't fair, either.

Erica was complicated. But she was also honest. He didn't have to doubt her intentions or wonder what she was thinking.

He was falling in love with her. He couldn't deny it anymore. But he also couldn't hang on to a fantasy that they could have a life together.

This morning proved it.

Erica did things her way, and he wasn't allowed to intervene. Plus, she'd hit a nerve when she'd accused him of not standing up to Haley.

She was right. He'd never stood up to his ex. Today was the closest he'd come to it. No one knew how hard it was for him to tell Haley what he really thought.

No wonder Erica thought he was a wimp.

Maybe he was.

He tossed the remote on the cushion next to him and stood. Stretched his arms behind his back to ease the tightness in his chest. Then crossed the room to the counter and uncovered the plate of cookies Gemma had given him. He popped a snickerdoodle into his mouth, barely noticing the cinnamon and sugar as he chewed.

He'd almost quit his job there on Erica's porch. But he needed this ranch too much.

Needed to ride Sugarpie every day. Needed to take care of the cattle and work alongside guys who listened to him. The paycheck was the least of it, but he needed that, too.

What he needed more than anything was an ounce of respect.

Maybe he should quit. Then he wouldn't have to worry that Erica was disappointed in him.

And maybe he should call Haley and tell her if Jamie ever showed up again, he was calling his lawyer. Then she'd listen.

The restlessness building inside him pulled him over to the window. Darkness had fallen, and the snow was piling up. He'd have to check the pregnant cows early in the morning. Make sure they were doing okay.

He turned away from the window to go sit back down on the couch. And hung his head.

God, I don't know what I'm doing wrong.

Canned laughter erupted from the television.

I'm more confused than ever. I've been happy here.

*And I've felt good about myself for the first time in years.
I thought…*

What? What had he thought?

He'd thought he and Erica had a good thing. A connection. Deeper feelings for each other. A chance at more.

The Christmas tree, with its buffalo-plaid ornaments and twinkling white lights, mocked him.

Maybe he hadn't been imagining their connection, but it didn't change the facts. He was in over his head with his boss, and she might like him, but she didn't respect him.

But other things ran through his head—all the afternoons going over the ranch checklist together. She listened to him, asked intelligent questions and trusted his opinion. She'd done it again and again.

That was respect.

Yeah, for my ranching skills.

He wanted her respect for him as a man. As *her* man.

Could he be her man?

Not if she wasn't going to listen to him. Not if she looked down on him.

He'd been there. Done that.

The pain and anger in her eyes when they'd stood in front of Haley and Jamie came back to him.

Could he be viewing this all wrong? He was convinced she wouldn't listen to him, that she didn't respect him. But they'd both been blindsided by their exes.

What had Erica needed in that moment?

His breath released in a whoosh. She'd needed him to be on her side. To support her. And he'd blown it.

All he'd wanted to do was defuse the situation and send Haley and Jamie on their way. And all she'd wanted was to prevent the situation from happening again.

Dalton had failed her.

And he'd failed himself, too.

Erica was right. Jamie and Haley expected both of them to put up with any inconvenience, any change of plans.

Pick her son up an hour early? Erica was told to lighten up.

Question why Haley was there when she shouldn't be? Erica was labeled a drama queen.

And when Dalton had entered the fray, Erica had defended him, only to be told by her ex that she was petty and predictable.

No wonder she'd been upset. No wonder she'd told Dalton she wasn't done. No wonder she'd been willing to verbally duke it out.

This was a woman who fought for herself and for her loved ones.

She would never back down.

He couldn't say the same for himself.

And it made the situation clear. He didn't deserve Erica Black. He never had.

"Well, you were right. Again." Erica tried to keep her tone light, but her heart was brittle and cracking. She sat on a stool at the counter surrounded by the pretty holly decorations that did absolutely nothing to improve her mood. "I fell for the wrong cowboy."

She'd surprised herself when she dialed her mom. After hours of reliving the morning's confrontation and trying to justify her actions, she'd surrendered to reality. Erica was hopeless when it came to men.

"Oh, no, why do you say that?" Her mom's sympathetic tone made her want to cry. And, surprisingly, she hadn't shed a tear all day.

"I got too close to Dalton, even when I knew it wasn't

smart. I mean, you said it best—our exes are always going to be around. I ignored it. And I regret it."

"Is he still in love with her?"

"No." She believed him, too. He didn't seem like a guy pining for his ex.

"Then what's the problem?"

Why wasn't her mom telling her "I told you so"?

"Jamie showed up an hour early to pick up Rowan. And he brought Haley with him. I let him have it, and he told me to lighten up and said I was a drama queen. Then Haley said something rude about me to Dalton, and he basically told her she'd taken everything from him and what more did she want? Then she or Jamie—I don't even remember at this point—said I only hired Dalton to get back at them, and I piped in that I hired him because he's the best rancher in the county. Well, Jamie claimed I did it to be petty and that I was predictable, at which point I said I was calling my lawyer."

As the words poured out of her mouth, she was struck by how stupid it all sounded.

Maybe she was a drama queen. She *did* need to lighten up. She *was* being petty and predictable.

"I am so sorry, Erica. I know how painful that must have been. I hope you called the lawyer."

Her throat clenched so tightly she was afraid her air supply was getting cut off, but when the tears began to slide down her cheeks, she found she could breathe again.

"I did. I left a message."

"What does this have to do with Dalton?"

"He broke up the argument. Told me to stop. I resented it. And then after the boys left, we argued."

"I see."

And there it was. The judgmental "I see" she'd expected. The one she deserved.

"It's okay to stand up for yourself, Erica. Jamie's not following court orders. You have every right to call him out on it."

"Mom, you don't have to sugarcoat it with me. I feel like every month that passes I get shriller and more immature when it comes to our custody arrangement."

"You have good reason to be."

"Yeah, but is having a good reason enough?" She pushed her hair away from her forehead. "I saw how I looked from Dalton's viewpoint, and I..." She wiped the tears from her face.

"You what?"

"I don't like myself. I don't like who I am when Jamie's around. I was mean and ugly. To everyone."

"Well, Erica, I like you all the time. Good, bad, mean, ugly. I love you. Always have. You have a big personality—and a big heart. You're not perfect. I'm not, either. It's okay. We don't have to be. We just keep trying our best."

The tears threatened to start spilling again. "You're only saying that because you're my mom."

"When have I ever told you what you wanted to hear?"

"That's true." Erica let out a half hiccup, half chuckle. Her nose was dripping—she reached over for a tissue and caught it in time.

"How deep are your feelings for Dalton?" her mom asked quietly.

"They're deep."

"Talk to him. You're not afraid of a confrontation. Find out how he feels. And listen to what he says."

That's what she was afraid of. What if she confronted

him and found out she'd been fooling herself? He could never love someone with a big mouth like her.

"I'll think about it." She chatted with her mom for a few more minutes. "Thanks, Mom. I love you."

"I love you, too."

They ended the call. Things she'd pushed away all day came back to her, and this time she paid attention.

To Dalton claiming Haley never listened to him. To him saying he'd disappointed his ex and would only disappoint her, too.

Is that what he thought? That Erica wouldn't listen to him? That she'd be disappointed in him?

The man listened to her and helped her with anything she asked, and not because he was her employee. Because he was the kind of guy who helped. The kind of guy who got things done and expected nothing in return.

He'd complimented her so many times on things that mattered to her—not her looks, but her personality. He saw the best in her, recognized her talents. He was the one to suggest opening an event center. He believed in her.

Dalton Cambridge was everything she'd ever wanted in a man.

And she'd been so blind with anger, she'd pushed him away.

Maybe he was right to tell her to take a few days to think.

He deserved to have a woman who listened to him, who respected him. As much as she wanted to be that woman, deep down she was afraid she'd proven Jamie right. She was a petty, vindictive drama queen.

She and Dalton had been clear with each other—neither could handle another divorce.

Erica wasn't easy to love. She wasn't the type of woman a guy stuck around for.

She didn't want to make Dalton's life miserable, too.

Chapter Thirteen

Man, it was cold out here. Dalton tucked his chin into his parka as he checked on the cattle. He'd already fed them, and now they were huddled together against the wind. Christmas Eve. Cold and windy and miserable. Just like him.

He'd slept in short bursts, waking up numerous times with a sinking feeling, until he'd finally gotten out of bed and come out here. Dawn had arrived a few hours ago, but the day was gray, and the wind blew in gusts.

Dalton directed Sugarpie back to the stables. Brushed and fed her. Then strode to the equipment shed to install a new wiper blade on the tractor. Maybe it would distract him from his jumbled thoughts. As he hunted through the boxes of parts, he tried to shush the questions racing through his mind.

What was Erica doing now? Was she mad at him? Had she called her lawyer? Should he call his?

Did she hate him?

And he forced his thoughts somewhere else—to Grady—which didn't help. Because all he could see was Grady's smiling face with his other family. Haley and Jamie and Rowan. The four of them would celebrate Christmas Eve today and wake up tomorrow to a tree and gifts and…Dalton wouldn't be there. He'd miss it. He had no choice in the matter.

It was as if he'd been cut out of his son's life. Replaced.

The new wiper blade caught his eye, and he snatched it out of the box. As soon as he was done in here, he was going to lick his wounded heart back at his cabin. He just needed to get through this miserable Christmas Eve somehow.

But as he climbed up the tractor and reached over to the windshield, he pictured Haley yesterday with Jamie's arm around her. How she hadn't listened to a single word Dalton had said.

He thought of all the extra money she demanded each month when he already paid her a large amount of money for child support.

He thought of how she'd shown up with Jamie instead of following their agreed upon plan.

His dejection flamed to anger. He gripped the new wiper blade in his hand. *God, I need some help here. I can't keep doing things Haley's way. I can't keep giving in.*

A Bible passage sprang to mind, one he'd memorized as a kid and read many times over the years. It was from John 14:27. "Peace I leave with you, my peace I give unto you: not as the world giveth, give I unto you. Let not your heart be troubled, neither let it be afraid."

Peace. Hmm…what would that be like? Peace would mean he didn't have a sinking sensation in his gut every time he got a call or text from his ex-wife. It would mean he didn't need to dread seeing Haley and Jamie together anymore, either.

God would give him peace. And part of that peace was

no longer putting up with stuff he shouldn't have been putting up with in the first place.

Haley had left him. She had a new husband, a new life. And that meant Dalton had a new life, too.

He was done with her games.

Abandoning the wiper, he climbed back down off the tractor. Pulled his phone out of his pocket and pressed Haley's number. She answered after a few rings.

"Hello?"

"Yesterday was unacceptable." He felt jittery but kept his tone even.

"I don't know what you're talking about."

"You were not supposed to be there."

"It wasn't a big deal," she said in a pinched voice.

"Maybe not to you, but it was to me. If you won't abide by our custody arrangement, I will contact my lawyer."

"Isn't that a little dramatic?" Her sarcasm held a touch of fear, and he softened. This was Christmas. The mother of his child. He wasn't trying to punish her. He simply wanted her to heed the rules they'd agreed on.

"No, it's not," he said. "Also, I pay you child support. Stop asking me for more money."

"Wow, Dalton. This is your son we're talking about." Her voice grew whispery at the end. He didn't care.

"Yes, it is. He's your son, too. If you want to buy him special suits and send him to an expensive preschool, that's your decision. I'm not shelling out extra money anymore."

"Well, merry Christmas to you, too, you grinch." Gone was the whisper. Something icy had taken its place.

Grinch? His mouth curved into a smile. A big smile. A happy smile. He'd rather be a grinch than a wimp.

"Merry Christmas, Haley. I'll see you tomorrow."

The resentment, the fear, the self-loathing—all gone.

All this time he'd been wrong about himself. Maybe he'd always considered Haley better than him. Over the years, she'd manipulated him with her martyr act and breathy voice. Even after the divorce, he'd believed he wasn't good enough for her.

And now he recognized the truth.

He'd always been good enough.

It was about time he appreciated himself. He didn't need to wait for anyone to come along and do it for him.

He slid the phone back into his pocket and climbed back on the tractor. Whistling a Christmas tune, he replaced the wiper, all thoughts of his ex-wife gone.

He had one more thing to do today.

Apologize to Erica.

He had no idea what to say or how to say it, but he needed to make things right with her.

There wasn't enough coffee in the world on this Christmas Eve.

Erica rolled out the sweet dough for the sticky buns with Gemma. They stood on opposite sides of the island. "Santa Baby" came through the wireless speakers, and she'd turned on all the lights, including the Christmas tree, in an attempt to brighten up the dreary day.

"You seem down today," Gemma said. "Are you missing Rowie?"

"Yeah, I am." She set aside the rolling pin. Her heart wasn't into baking. "But I'm still upset about yesterday."

Gemma made a clucking sound with her tongue as she chopped pecans. "Jamie shouldn't have brought her here."

"I agree." She sighed. "But I also should have done

a better job of keeping my temper in check. I'm mad at myself."

"He was very rude. You couldn't help it." Her kind eyes and sweet smile made Erica feel even worse. What had she ever done to deserve this dear woman in her life?

"Yes, but I'm used to it. It wasn't the first time he called me a drama queen. Petty and predictable—that's me." She lifted her gaze to the ceiling momentarily. "For once, I agree with him. He's right."

Gemma set down the knife and wagged her finger to Erica. "None of that. No beating yourself up. Not today. It's Christmas Eve."

"I need to change." Erica pressed her fingers into her temples.

"No, you don't, honey. You're perfect the way you are."

While she'd like to agree, she couldn't.

"Gemma, I'm serious. This anger and lashing out every time Jamie does things his way isn't good for me. And it's not good for Rowan, either. I have to find a way to be around Jamie and Haley for my son's sake. He should be able to be in the same room with all of us without getting his stomach tied into knots worrying we'll start fighting. We've kept him from our animosity for the most part, but he's getting older."

"I see your point." She returned to her spot and resumed chopping the nuts. "What are you going to do about it?"

"I don't know."

"Sleigh Ride" came through the speakers, and its happy beat was completely out of sync with her sad heart.

"Well, I'm not the best person to offer advice," Gemma said. "I do read my Bible, though, and I know you do, too. There have been many times in my life when I should have been praying, but I wasn't. I wish I would have prayed more after Bob died. I felt lost and mad at God, and it's no secret my life fell apart. I let it fall apart."

"I'm sorry, Gemma. I know that was a terrible time for you."

She nodded, looking sad. "I still don't pray the way I should, but I'll tell you this. I thank the Good Lord every day for you and Rowan."

"I thank Him for you, too, Gemma. I don't know what I would do without you."

They went back to their tasks, with Gemma mixing brown sugar and cinnamon together. Erica finished rolling out the dough, then excused herself for a moment. She strode down the hall to her bedroom and shut the door. And sank onto the edge of the bed.

Lord, Gemma is right about praying. Please forgive me for my resentment, my anger and my need to punish Jamie. I don't want to be like this anymore. There must be a way I can be around them without my temper flaring. Will You help me?

She didn't sense any change. Nothing felt different.

What had she expected? A burning bush in her bedroom or something?

God, I'm just going to keep praying every day. I'm going to trust You with this, because I cannot do it on my own. And Mom always tells me Your timing is perfect. So if it takes a month, a year, ten years or a lifetime, I'm going to keep praying about it.

She sat a few minutes before rising and walking to the door. And the other big issue she'd been grappling with came to mind front and center.

Dalton.

He'd seen her at her worst yesterday. She wasn't sure

how they were going to get past it. All she knew was that she'd fallen for him and blown it.

She was ashamed of herself.

She'd never be demure and classy like Haley…

No. She wasn't going down that road. She'd compared herself to that woman enough.

What had her mother said yesterday about not being perfect?

Erica *couldn't* be perfect. Didn't have it in her. And today, of all days, held all the proof she didn't need to be. Christmas was about celebrating the birth of a Savior— her Savior. True God. True man. Perfect so she didn't have to be. Perfect because she couldn't be.

As she reentered the kitchen, her heart felt lighter. "Okay, what else needs to be done?"

Gemma gave her a big smile. "Sprinkle the cinnamon sugar over the dough, and then we'll roll it up."

She'd take today one minute at a time. But at some point, she needed to figure out the Dalton situation. He was important to her. She didn't want to let him go.

But she might not have a choice in the matter.

Chapter Fourteen

As dusk fell that night, Dalton ignored the chill in the air as he strode to Erica's house. Gemma had waved to him from the front window of her cabin when he passed by. Good. It meant Erica was alone. He hoped she'd be willing to hear him out.

After his call with Haley, Dalton had gone back to his cabin and showered. He'd fought with himself for a long time trying to figure out what to say to Erica.

He needed a grand gesture. But he didn't have any up his sleeve.

The stores were all closed for the holidays, and he wouldn't know what to buy beyond roses and candy, anyhow. Maybe it was better this way. He was a simple man. Not a grand-gesture type of guy.

He could become one, though, for Erica. She made anything seem possible.

Before meeting her, he'd had little hope for the future, and after meeting her, he'd become alive again.

Right now, he had high hopes for the future. With her in it. Which was why his nerves were shot and he had no idea how this conversation would go.

Dalton took the porch steps two at a time and stamped his boots on her welcome mat. Took a deep breath. And knocked.

The seconds ticked by, and then the door opened, and his jaw fell to the ground.

Erica was all dressed up in a red dress and high heels. Her hair fell in neat waves around her shoulders, and her subtle makeup made her even more gorgeous than she already was.

But it was her smile—her glossy, red-stained-lips, glorious smile—that melted him.

"You're here." Her eyes began to sparkle.

"I am."

"Good." She took him by the hand and dragged him inside. He took it as a good sign. She easily could have demanded he get off her porch. "We have to talk."

"I agree." He made quick work of removing his boots and hanging his coat on the closet handle. They made their way down the hall to the living room, and he noted the mellow instrumental Christmas music and dimmed lighting that made the Christmas tree lights shine even brighter.

"Why are you so dressed up?" He gravitated to the tree as she took a seat on the sectional.

"I got ready early. I decided to skip the children's service and try the candlelight one instead."

He almost smacked his forehead. He'd forgotten about the Christmas Eve service tonight. Here he'd been praying all day, and God had shown him mercy by helping him get his head on straight. Shouldn't his priority be worshipping in church?

Well, it wasn't too late. But for now…

"I owe you an apology," he said, turning to face her. "For yesterday."

"No, you don't." Erica crossed one leg over the other and let her forearm rest along the length of the sectional's arm.

"Yes, I do." He took a seat next to her, making sure he left space between them. "I'm not excusing my actions, but I need you to know where I was coming from."

She tilted her head to the side and watched him.

"I've spent years on eggshells around Haley. Until recently, I wasn't aware of it. I just knew something was wrong, and that I was the problem. Her subtle disapproval had me scrambling to make her happy. Even after our divorce. If she needs money for something for Grady, I fork it over. If she needs pick-up times changed, I do it. And yesterday, well, having Jamie there with her was my worst fear come true. They both look down on me. And, to be honest, I get it. I understand why they do. Haley grew up with money, and Jamie did, too. I didn't."

"Well, I think that's ridiculous. It doesn't matter how much money you grew up with or how much you have now." Her eyes flashed.

"It's okay." He held his hand out in defense. "I've finally acknowledged it. I've been ignoring my own role in the situation. And it's high time I change how I deal with it."

Erica lowered her lashes.

"Yesterday when they arrived, I should have supported you. I hate that they were so disrespectful to you, and I hate that I allowed them to get away with it. I wanted to make the situation go away, but you were right. It never goes away. They keep taking more and more, and I let them. I allow Haley to walk all over me."

"Dalton, I—"

"Just hear me out, and I promise you can have the floor and say every last thing on your mind. But let me spill the rest first."

She nodded.

"I called her today."

"Haley?"

"Yeah." He opened his hands. "I told her the next time she doesn't follow our agreement I'm contacting my lawyer. I mean it, too. I'm done with her games. I also told her I pay child support for a reason, and she would have to pay for Grady's extra expenses with that. I'm done being her ATM."

Erica's stunned expression motivated him to continue.

"Here's the thing, Erica. I wasn't mean about it. I didn't get upset. She tried to argue with me, and I didn't take the bait, nor did I slink away and let her win. It felt good. It felt so good, I honestly think I could handle being in the same room with her and Jamie without being overwhelmed by a feeling of inadequacy anymore. And it's all because of you."

"Me?" She splayed her hands across her chest. "What did I do?"

"You showed me it's okay to stand up for myself. That confrontation is messy, but it's worth it. Sometimes it's necessary."

"Dalton, you never had any reason to feel inadequate around them."

"I know that now." He gave her a tender smile. "Do you remember when you walked into the feedstore?"

"How could I forget?"

"You looked so confident. So utterly sure of yourself."

"I did?"

"Yeah. You did. And I thought you were like them—

like Haley and Jamie. I thought you'd look down on me
or you were trying to use me for some revenge thing."

"Not my style." She brushed her hand off her shoulder.

"I know that now. You're the type of person who doesn't
avoid sticky situations. You see something that needs to
be done, and you do it. I admire that about you. I admire
a lot about you."

"Hold that thought." Erica held out her index finger.
Her eyes were round and unsure.

He frowned. Was this where she told him she'd come
to her senses after their fight yesterday? That she was
the boss and he was the manager, and she didn't have
feelings for him?

The conversation had been going well. But...he braced
himself for the worst. He deserved it, after all.

"There's nothing to admire about me, Dalton. I've been
so ashamed of myself ever since they left." Erica couldn't
believe this incredible man had ever felt inadequate. And
he'd overlooked all her flaws. He was even compliment-
ing her.

"It's funny—" she stared at the Christmas tree for a
moment before redirecting her attention to him "—but
you and I are actually a lot alike when it comes to our
exes. You said they made you feel inadequate. That sums
it up for me, too. Haley is a classic beauty. Quiet. She
dresses impeccably and seems like a nice enough person."

Dalton grunted.

"I'm nothing like her. I am not quiet or classy. I ride
horses and smell like the stables half the time. If I'm not
wearing jeans and a sweater, I'm in joggers. I'm loud.
And honestly, I'm not a nice person. I'm not."

"You are." His eyes gleamed.

"Uh, no. I shoot my mouth off without thinking how my words will affect people. I have limited self-control when it comes to my ex. You saw it for yourself. I get so angry when he pulls these stupid stunts. I act like a child around him. I'm like a little kid throwing a temper tantrum."

"I don't see it that way."

"I have to change. Because you were right yesterday. Jamie isn't going to." She shook her head. "I'm only hurting myself. I can't keep overreacting to him and Haley. Rowan's little now. It's easy to keep him in the house or another room when they come around. But the day will be coming when we'll be forced to be together for school plays and sports, and it's not fair for him to have warring parents. I can't do that to him. I won't. Not anymore."

"What are you saying?"

Her heart felt like it had been ripped open and was bleeding after she'd admitted all that. But she inhaled and continued. "I need to change, Dalton. I can feel it in my bones. This angry, in-your-face version of me isn't who I am. It isn't who I want to be."

"Who do you want to be?"

"Someone quiet. Classy." She hadn't realized how much she meant it until the words came out of her mouth. And to her surprise, tears formed in her eyes. "I want to be nice. I want to be better."

Dalton stood then and held his hand out to her. She placed hers in his and allowed him to help her to her feet.

"Being quiet and classy are overrated. They don't make a person good. You're good, Erica. You're the nicest, most generous person I know." He held both of her hands in his. "Didn't you ever hear the expression 'actions speak louder than words'?"

She blinked away the tears. Dalton's tender expression and his low voice made her lower lip tremble. She'd yearned for the words he was saying, yet she didn't quite believe them.

He tipped her chin to look into his eyes. And her breath caught at the intensity in his.

"Erica…" Her name was a caress. "You are vitality in a bottle. You walk in a room and the air shifts. You bring energy and excitement to everything you do. Look at the legacy club. And the Christmas festival. You have a gift—it's the gift of hope. I look at you, and you make me feel like I can do anything. You believe in yourself and your projects, and in turn, you help others believe in themselves, too. You're a role model, and I don't think you even know it."

Her tears began to fall. How she'd craved hearing words like that her entire life. Her family had always accepted and loved her. But no one had ever spelled out her good qualities the way Dalton just had.

"God gave you leadership skills, Erica." His hands caressed her arms. "He made you loud and bold and spectacular. I don't feel worthy of you, but I can't let you go. I don't know how anyone could ever let you go. I love you."

Her breath caught in her throat. Her? He loved her?

"I don't blame you if you don't feel the same." He frowned. "I know you need a man who will stand by your side and fight your battles alongside you. I wasn't that man yesterday. But, Erica, I could be. I want to be."

"You mean it, don't you?" She probed his eyes, needing to be sure. "You really do love me?"

"I do." His firm nod was all it took.

"I love you, too. I'll take your love. Oh, Dalton, I'll take it. And you're wrong about yourself. You've been standing beside me ever since moving here. You're the support I've always needed and never had. I appreciate the fact that you're willing to step away from a situation instead of escalating it."

"And I appreciate you for sticking up for what's right." He pulled her closer, and her heart felt ready to explode with fireworks.

"You give me courage. Look at the pole barn—you knew my dreams before I did. An event center is the perfect business—for me, for the barn and for Jewel River."

"Right back at you. This ranch is my dream come true." His mouth kicked into a lopsided smile. "You really love me?"

"Yes, you goofball." She swatted his arm.

"I don't have much to offer you. I've got about five bucks in the bank. I do have the best horse on the planet, though." His hands slipped around her waist, and the heat in his gaze warmed her more than a mug of hot cocoa ever could.

"I don't have much to offer you, either," she teased. "Well, besides this massive ranch. I guess I could let you ride Murphy, the best horse on the planet."

He laughed and she joined him, then the mood shifted, and she knew he wanted to kiss her as much as she wanted him to kiss her.

And then he did.

She sank into his embrace. This man saw only the best in her, and she wanted him to know how much she loved him, how much she valued him. As he deepened the kiss, she was overcome with a sense of awe.

Dalton was the man she'd been looking for all her life. The man who accepted and appreciated her. The one who would be by her side, supporting her. The man she needed.

When they finally broke away, Dalton continued to hold her close and looked into her eyes. "What now?"

"We date."

"When?"

"Tonight." She placed her finger against his lips. "You're taking me to the Christmas Eve service."

"When is it again?" He was standing so close his breath was warm against her cheek.

"Not for another hour."

"Plenty of time."

"For what?"

"For this." And he kissed her again.

Chapter Fifteen

This was the best Christmas ever.

Dalton sat on Erica's couch with his arm slung over her shoulders the following afternoon. He'd picked up Grady earlier and told Haley that he and Erica were dating. As expected, she'd been upset, but he'd simply waved to her and wished her a merry Christmas. Erica had told Jamie, too, and she'd walked away without reacting as he'd called out nasty things to her. Progress.

After he and Grady had opened presents in his cabin, Dalton had carried him on his shoulders through the freshly fallen snow. He and Erica had agreed to let the boys play for a while before driving up to Sunrise Bend for Erica's family's Christmas party, which she'd insisted he attend with her.

She hadn't had to insist too hard. He liked her family. Wanted to hang out with them.

"I'm surprised Gemma hasn't stopped by yet." He worried about her sometimes. As much as she loved the boys and seemed content to stay on the ranch, she withdrew and got melancholy, too. "I custom-ordered our movie shirts, but they won't be here for two more weeks."

"I'll call her again." Erica patted his hand, then stood, swiped her phone off the end table and called.

He kept one eye on the boys, who were both on the floor on their tummies, legs kicking behind them, as they raced their new cars around a track. Every now and then one of them would let out a shout, or they'd both giggle hysterically. He couldn't get enough of watching them play together.

"Yes, come over…Dalton's here…we have something to tell you…"

He cocked his head to hear the rest of their conversation, but Erica had ended the call and was standing there beaming. "She's coming over."

"Good."

Then Erica sat down next to him, snuggling up against his side, and he couldn't help thinking how right this was. For weeks, a relationship with her had seemed all wrong. And now? It was the most natural thing in the world to sit here on Christmas Day and watch their sons play together.

Last night they'd held hands as they walked into church, and people had noticed. He and Erica agreed it made no sense to hide it. They loved each other, and nothing was going to change their feelings. But they wanted Gemma to hear it from them.

The song "Rockin' Around the Christmas Tree" started playing, and Erica grimaced, lurching to her feet. "Ugh, this song."

"Wock, twee!" Rowan scrambled to stand up and started shaking his hips.

And Dalton knew exactly what would make the day even better.

"Come on, Grady and Rowan, let's dance." Dalton

stood and held his hands out. The boys ran to him. The three of them held hands and began shimmying right there next to the tree.

Erica's face broke into a big grin and she joined their circle, taking one of Rowan's hands and one of Grady's in hers.

"Wock, twee, Mama!"

"Yes, sir." She laughed. "Let's rock around this Christmas tree."

They all danced, laughing until they were out of breath.

"Well, this is a nice surprise." Gemma clapped her hands. "Merry Christmas!"

"Mewwy Chwistmas, Gwammy Gemma!" Rowan let go of Erica's hand and launched himself into Gemma's arms. Grady sprinted over, too, and they both clung to her legs.

"Oh, my boys." Looking teary-eyed, she leaned over to hug them both. "My two sweethearts."

"See my new twuck?" Rowan pointed to the toys on the floor.

"Mine, too!" Grady said.

The boys ran off to get their toys, and Dalton put his arm around Erica's shoulders.

"Gemma, we have something to tell you." Erica looked up at Dalton.

"You're in love!" Gemma opened her arms wide and hugged them both. "I knew you were right for each other. Daltie, Erica's your secret Santa, and Erica, he's your Mr. Right. I just knew you'd figure it out."

Secret Santa? Mr. Right? Dalton shook his head. Gemma had been watching too many of those movies. He didn't mind one bit.

Erica blinked a few times then grinned and shrugged. "Okay."

"See? Gwammy Gemma?" Rowan and Grady held their new trucks up to her, and she took the opportunity to sit in her chair as they told her all about their Christmas presents. Erica excused herself to get a plate of sticky buns for them to snack on.

Dalton took it all in. He, Gemma and Erica had found a family together. And here in this living room full of Christmas spirit, with the sound of laughter and Christmas songs, he'd found a place where he truly belonged.

"What's this I hear about you wanting to buy a pony?"

Erica sat next to her dad on the couch in her parents' living room that evening. Mom, Reagan, Holly and Sienna were in the dining room coloring with the kids, while Jet, Blaine and Dalton had gone out to the stables so Jet could show off his new horse. Erica had taken the opportunity to speak to her dad alone. They were sipping warm apple cider in front of the tall Christmas tree.

"I didn't say a pony." She raised her index finger. "More like a small, gentle horse for Rowan and Grady to learn how to ride."

"You know what I think?" His eyes twinkled, and Erica smiled. What a change from a few years ago, when her father had been sad and withdrawn after finding out her younger brother had died.

"What?"

"I think two horses are better than one," he said. "That way the boys can learn together."

She liked the idea. Could picture them riding around a paddock together. "Dalton might not go for it."

"Leave it to me and your brothers. We'll take care of Dalton." He patted her knee. "He'll come around."

Erica chuckled. "He doesn't know what he's getting into, does he?"

"We're glad to have him." Dad smiled. "You found someone worthy of you, honey."

The compliment sank in. Her dad usually didn't say things like this.

"Thank you, Dad."

"I mean it. I stayed out of your relationship with Jamie, and sometimes I wonder if I should have spoken up."

"If it makes you feel better, I doubt I would have listened to you. And, well, if I had, then we wouldn't have gotten married, and I wouldn't have Rowan."

"True." He nodded thoughtfully. "I wish I could have spared you the pain, though."

"I learned from it. I'm still learning from it." She realized it was true. The hard times had shaped her into who she was today. And the things she learned today would shape who she became tomorrow.

"Now, Dalton? He's a trustworthy man. A good cowboy. He'll make you a fine husband someday."

"Whoa, there." She held her hands out. "We aren't talking marriage. We just realized we love each other. Give us twenty-four hours at least."

"You? My headstrong girl?" He grinned. "I'll give you forty-eight hours. Tops."

She couldn't help laughing. Then she scooted closer to him and leaned her head on his shoulder. "Thanks, Dad. I love you."

"I love you, too."

A commotion from the other room had them exchanging glances. They both got up and headed to the kitchen, where laughter and loud voices combined.

The guys had come back in, and the kids were surrounding them.

"Duck, duck, goose?" Jet was on one knee talking to his five-year-old, Clara. "That's too much running for an old guy like me."

"Please, Daddy?" Her little hands were in the prayer position as she pleaded with him.

"Daddy, duck, duck?" Maddie—Blaine's daughter, Madeline—clapped her hands.

Then Grady and Rowan started getting into it, yelling, "Duck, duck," and Erica's lips twitched with laughter as her brothers and Dalton caved to the kids and began herding them into the family room. Dalton stopped in the doorway, where she was standing while everyone else continued on their way.

"Have I told you this has been the best Christmas ever?" He drew her close, wrapping his arms around her waist, his face inches from hers.

"No, but I agree. It's been pretty spectacular." She smoothed the front of his shirt, marveling at the strong muscles beneath.

"You know what else is pretty spectacular?"

She smiled up at him, shaking her head.

"You." He nodded as his eyes shimmered with love. "I love you, Erica Black. Thanks for making me and Grady part of the family today."

"Not just today, cowboy. Ready or not, you're part of the family. And if that thought doesn't terrify you, I don't know what will."

He laughed, then leaned down to kiss her. It was a light kiss, soft and full of promise.

"Merry Christmas, Erica."

"Merry Christmas, Daltie."

"If we're going to be together, we need rules." He gently pushed her hair behind her ear.

"Oh, yeah? What kind of rules?"

"No calling me Daltie."

She slid her hands around his neck. "Okay, Big D."

"How about plain old Dalton?"

"Eh, I'll have to think about it." She reached up to kiss him.

"Okay, I don't care what you want me to call you, as long as you're mine."

"That's what I was hoping for, Big D."

Epilogue

"Everyone please take a seat, and we'll get this meeting started." Erica stood at the head of the table in the church's all-purpose room on a blustery evening in March. The community center wouldn't be completely repaired for a few more months, and in the meantime, the Jewel River Legacy Club was meeting at the church. As the members—some old, some new—found their seats, she reflected on everything that had happened since Christmas.

Her life was full of unexpected blessings.

The best one was sitting right next to her. Dalton had decided to join the legacy club now that they were officially engaged. On Saturday, he'd asked her to marry him with help from Gemma and a little advice from her mother. He'd done good. She peeked at the pretty engagement ring on her finger. He'd done good, indeed.

After Clem led them in reciting the pledge and saying the Lord's Prayer, Erica asked everyone to sit.

"Before we get started, I have something to share." She glanced at Dalton and practically melted with love on the spot. "Dalton and I are engaged."

A round of congratulations erupted around the table.

Clem rolled his eyes. "Like we didn't know already. We saw you in church with the ring on."

"Not everyone was there, Clem." Christy glared at him. "It wouldn't kill you to be happy for them."

"I'll be happy when we get to Angela's flag presentation so we can vote no on it once and for all."

"Just wait until you see the presentation." Angela Zane, undeterred by Clem's rudeness, beamed. "You're going to vote yes. My grandson added special effects and everything. He even made flames come out of the sky behind it. It's exciting."

"Good gravy, someone save me." Clem shook his head, his hand cupped to his forehead.

"Before we get to that—" Christy threw a glare Clem's way "—I want to personally congratulate Erica and Dalton. Will your wedding be the first event in your new barn after the renovations are complete?"

"We'll have to see." Erica had gotten the permits to convert the pole barn into an event center, and she and Dalton decided to call it The Winston in honor of her great-aunt and uncle.

"If not, maybe one of my boys—" Christy turned to give a pointed stare to Cade "—will take your lead and find brides. You're not getting any younger, son."

A wicked smile grew on Cade's face. "Then who would drive you around town, Ma? Couldn't have a girlfriend distracting me from my chauffer duties."

"My license was reinstated two months ago." Christy glowered at him.

"Yeah, and you got pulled over again on Friday."

"The sheriff let me go with a warning. It wasn't my fault that traffic cone was in the wrong spot."

Clem let out a whistle and pointed to Cade. "You got nerves of steel, boy, I'll give you that."

Erica needed to get the meeting back on track. And quickly.

"Marc, maybe you could let us know where we're at on finding ways to fill the empty downtown buildings?"

Marc Young nodded and launched into his report.

Dalton covered her hand with his own and leaned over, then whispered, "You're good at this."

She glanced at him, flashing him a quick grin. "Thanks."

"Think your sister will like it here?" he whispered.

"I know she will." Erica had finally convinced Reagan to move here next month when her chocolate gig in Denver was finished.

The meeting continued—Angela's presentation had multiple special effects, including explosions and lightning flashes, which drew a round of applause—and finally, it was over.

Johnny Abbot approached her as Dalton excused himself to talk to Cade about his stables.

"Erica?" Johnny said. "Can I ask you something?"

"Sure, Johnny, what's on your mind?" She gathered her notes into a folder.

"I wanted to ask you about…" His blue eyes clouded under his glasses, and he held a cowboy hat between his hands.

She gave him her full attention. "It's okay. You can ask me anything."

"Well, it's about… Gemma Redmond. We went to school together, and I…I'd like to pay her a visit. She was real kind to me back then."

"Oh, Johnny, that's awfully nice of you. Gemma, well,

she keeps to herself mostly. Why don't I give you her number, and you can contact her?"

He smiled. "Yes, I'll give her a call."

"Here you go." She wrote down Gemma's number, hoping the woman wouldn't mind.

After taking it, Johnny smiled at her again and tucked the paper into his pocket before walking away.

Then Dalton approached. "Are you ready?"

"I think so."

They followed the rest of the members out the door into the cold night.

"I think Christy Moulten's on to something," Dalton said as they made their way to his truck. "Our wedding could be the opening event for The Winston."

"It would only give us a few months to plan, though."

"Exactly." He stopped in front of the passenger door and turned her to face him. "The sooner, the better."

"I like the way you're thinking."

"I like everything about you." He slid his hands behind her back.

"A summer wedding it is." She took his collar in her hands and gave him her biggest smile.

"The earlier, the better."

"You're speaking my language. Now let's start planning it."

"Right now?" He grinned.

She laughed, shivering. "Drive me home, cowboy. We'll talk on the way."

"You got it, boss."

* * * * *

Dear Reader,

Welcome to Jewel River! I'm delighted you picked up this book—the first in the new Wyoming Legacies series. Prepare to see a lot more of these characters in future books.

When I got the idea for Erica and Dalton to fall in love, I worried it was too out there for me to explore. Exes of exes? Talk about complicated. However, the sassy go-getter and easygoing rancher were perfect for each other. They just didn't know it. They needed time and a working relationship to truly understand how to get past the lingering effects of their divorces and to embrace a new life.

Like Erica, I find myself not always loving my personality. I say the wrong thing and regret it. I get stuck in one way of thinking and struggle to move on. But she's so lovable, and God helped her see herself the way He sees her—as His beloved child.

He sees you that way, too. If you're struggling with anything—a situation out of your control, feeling guilty about the past, wishing you had qualities you lack—give it to God. He'll help you see yourself as utterly loved and accepted by Him.

I love connecting with readers. Feel free to email me at jill@jillkemerer.com or write me at P.O. Box 2802, Whitehouse, Ohio, 43571.

Have the merriest of Christmases!
Jill Kemerer

COMING NEXT MONTH FROM
Love Inspired

THE AMISH MIDWIFE'S BARGAIN
by Patrice Lewis
After a tragic loss, midwife Miriam Kemp returns to her Amish roots and vows to leave her nursing life behind—until she accidentally hits Aaron Lapp with her car. Determined to make amends, she offers to help the reclusive Amish bachelor with his farm. Working together could open the door to healing... *and* love.

THE AMISH CHRISTMAS PROMISE
by Amy Lillard
Samuel Byler made a promise to take care of his late twin's family. He returns to his Amish community to honor that oath and marry Mattie Byler—only she wants nothing to do with him. But as Samuel proves he's a changed man, can obligation turn to love this Christmas?

HER CHRISTMAS HEALING
K-9 Companions • by Mindy Obenhaus
Shaken after an attack, Jillian McKenna hopes that moving to Hope Crossing, Texas, will help her find peace...and create a home for her baby-to-be. But her next-door neighbor, veterinarian Gabriel Vaughn, and his gentlehearted support dog might be the Christmas surprise Jillian's not expecting...

A WEDDING DATE FOR CHRISTMAS
by Kate Keedwell
Going to a Christmas Eve wedding solo is the last thing high school rivals Elizabeth Brennan and Mark Hayes want—especially when it's their exes tying the knot. The solution? They could pretend to date. After all, they've got nothing to lose...except maybe their hearts.

A FAMILY FOR THE ORPHANS
by Heidi Main
Following the death of their friends, Trisha Campbell comes to Serenity, Texas, to help cowboy Walker McCaw with the struggling farm and three children left in Walker's care. Now they have only the summer to try to turn things around for everyone—or risk losing the farm *and* each other.

THE COWGIRL'S LAST RODEO
by Tabitha Bouldin
Callie Wade's rodeo dreams are suspended when her horse suddenly goes blind. Their only chance to compete again lies with Callie's ex—horse trainer Brody Jacobs—who still hasn't forgotten how she broke his heart. Can working together help them see their way to the winner's circle...and a second chance?

_____

LICNM1023

Get 3 FREE REWARDS!

We'll send you 2 FREE Books plus a FREE Mystery Gift.

FREE Value Over **$20**

Both the **Love Inspired®** and **Love Inspired® Suspense** series feature compelling novels filled with inspirational romance, faith, forgiveness and hope.

YES! Please send me 2 FREE novels from the Love Inspired or Love Inspired Suspense series and my FREE gift (gift is worth about $10 retail). After receiving them, if I don't wish to receive any more books, I can return the shipping statement marked "cancel." If I don't cancel, I will receive 6 brand-new Love Inspired Larger-Print books or Love Inspired Suspense Larger-Print books every month and be billed just $6.49 each in the U.S. or $6.74 each in Canada. That is a savings of at least 16% off the cover price. It's quite a bargain! Shipping and handling is just 50¢ per book in the U.S. and $1.25 per book in Canada.* I understand that accepting the 2 free books and gift places me under no obligation to buy anything. I can always return a shipment and cancel at any time by calling the number below. The free books and gift are mine to keep no matter what I decide.

Choose one:
- ☐ **Love Inspired Larger-Print** (122/322 BPA GRPA)
- ☐ **Love Inspired Suspense Larger-Print** (107/307 BPA GRPA)
- ☐ **Or Try Both!** (122/322 & 107/307 BPA GRRP)

Name (please print)

Address _____ Apt. #

City _____ State/Province _____ Zip/Postal Code

Email: Please check this box ☐ if you would like to receive newsletters and promotional emails from Harlequin Enterprises ULC and its affiliates. You can unsubscribe anytime.

Mail to the Harlequin Reader Service:
IN U.S.A.: P.O. Box 1341, Buffalo, NY 14240-8531
IN CANADA: P.O. Box 603, Fort Erie, Ontario L2A 5X3

Want to try 2 free books from another series? Call 1-800-873-8635 or visit www.ReaderService.com.

*Terms and prices subject to change without notice. Prices do not include sales taxes, which will be charged (if applicable) based on your state or country of residence. Canadian residents will be charged applicable taxes. Offer not valid in Quebec. This offer is limited to one order per household. Books received may not be as shown. Not valid for current subscribers to the Love Inspired or Love Inspired Suspense series. All orders subject to approval. Credit or debit balances in a customer's account(s) may be offset by any other outstanding balance owed by or to the customer. Please allow 4 to 6 weeks for delivery. Offer available while quantities last.

Your Privacy—Your information is being collected by Harlequin Enterprises ULC, operating as Harlequin Reader Service. For a complete summary of the information we collect, how we use this information and to whom it is disclosed, please visit our privacy notice located at corporate.harlequin.com/privacy-notice. From time to time we may also exchange your personal information with reputable third parties. If you wish to opt out of this sharing of your personal information, please visit readerservice.com/consumerschoice or call 1-800-873-8635. **Notice to California Residents**—Under California law, you have specific rights to control and access your data. For more information on these rights and how to exercise them, visit corporate.harlequin.com/california-privacy.

LIRLIS23

HARLEQUIN
PLUS

Try the best multimedia subscription service for romance readers like you!

Read, Watch and Play.

Experience the easiest way to get the romance content you crave.

Start your **FREE TRIAL** at
<u>www.harlequinplus.com/freetrial</u>.